MW01322618

Only Fools Still Breathe

Only Fools Still Breathe

Suffer Little Children—
The Sweeter Potions of Life
Comes out of Jonestown

Lynette Vines Calvert

ISBN:	Hardcover	978-1-4415-5635-6
	Softcover	978-1-4415-5427-7

This book was printed in the United States of America.

To order additional copies of this book, contact:
Xlibris Corporation
1-888-795-4274
www.Xlibris.com
Orders@Xlibris.com
40757

CONTENTS

Dedication

To my husband, Kevin Lamont Calvert Sr.
To my sister: Deborah Cheryl Vines, and my cousin, Rosa Marie Staggers.
To my children:
Denise Marlene Calvert, Ashley Nicole Calvert, Theresa Dorthea Calvert, Kevin Lamont Calvert Jr., Lynette Renee Calvert II, and Mark Anthony Jones.
To the general public who knowingly and unknowingly helped to make this book possible.

Preface

You Bastard! These are the words that shot from my scorched tongue as I threw my cup of Coke against the wall above the 52-inch television screen one morning after I turned on a religious channel in my living room. I had just heard one of the television ministers tell a story about a child pornography ring. In this situation, the acoustics in my living room got as hazy and fuzzy as I needed them to be. For what seemed like the millionth time, I listened to the words "child sexual abuse." It seems as though each time that I heard of a situation concerning child sexual abuse, I grew angrier and angrier. This particular morning, I was about to explode with rage.
The television minister spoke of a little girl no more than four or five years old, who had been handcuffed, naked, and bound to a bed. The child was screaming in excruciating pain as a naked adult male lay behind her, brutally raping her again and again. Hearing this story shattered my heart into a million pieces, how about yours? I kept thinking about my mom's late cousin Glenda who was in her early thirties and always left babysitting us children. I was six, and my cousin Elijah was seven. Elijah's brother Rick-Rick was eight. Glenda used to make me sit and watch as she performed many types of indecent sexual acts with these little boys. I thought about tomjack (Skillet Brown), and many, many other child sexual abusers with whom I had come into contact within my life. I thought about how sex offender registries all throughout the United States report an astounding number of child victims each day.

Anyway, how did I handle this situation? The same way that I do now. I picked up my handy pen and began to create versatile stories and poetry as a pacifying outlet. Each creative poem and fiction story in this book was composed as a result of my exposure to child sexual abuse. Today, it is time to put down the pen and take a more positive and universal stand to combat child sexual abuse. For this reason, I have created a club to do just this. Together, we, from all walks of life, can do it if we are bold enough to bind together rather than throw our cups of Coke upside our walls, calling this situation a damn shame or grabbing our pen and creating literature as an outlet. This book is a call for professionals, lay public, and anyone who cares to help put a stop to all this child sexual abuse. Join my CSA club, and let's fight the hell out of child sexual abuse. If we pull together, we can make it happen. This is where it all starts and restarts. So much in the area of child sexual abuse has already been done, but so much more can be done. Do we hold our breaths and wait? If we are wise, yes we do, because if we hold our breaths and wait, the problem of child sexual abuse will get fixed much faster. In this case, "only fools still breathe." During the course of each breath that we take, more of our youths suffer senselessly. The children of the People's Temple in Jonestown could have possibly had a better escape route than our sexually abused youths. Let us gather together and change this. I have a strategy that I am convinced will work. Let us pull together and make it happen. Contact me at deniseandlynette@gmail.com

May God bless always,
Lynette Vines Calvert

One Last Dance with Thomas

In the shallow hours of the morning,
I age and watch old men love young women.
A pity it is that my curdling brows drip with arthritic and
ex-Miss America menopause.
Still, like mature cheese, I swell with a temperate freshness in this life.
And know that I know a place where I can crack my knees
and still model brown thighs

We call it the chicken bones of heaven on the outskirts
of a sweet Jewish hell
It is a place that I made one day in and of my horizoned youngness
In the wee mornings, I see old men longing on isolated
shores for the love of young girls
It's a sin that my botoxed fingers can no longer
stroke soft gray eyes and blond toupees

Nonetheless I know a place where I can sway my corroded hips
by sea light in the city.
I know a place where calm pheasants do romantically dance
for young senior citizens.
May I take you to where youthful orange cardinals love
humped backs and pinched noses.
In the sweets of God, there is an altar that leads us aged to
the graceful stairs of infinity.

Before my cart leaves this betrayal of youth,
I wanna dance, dine, and grind with youth.
I wanna be a part of the complexity that teary old men
desire in young women with age.
In creases of the morning, I age and watch old men love
young girls who love all men.
But, lo, I know that I know an orbit in my geriatric heart
is as certain as God's Thomas.

VENICE IS RISING

Robust bouquets and pink ribbons above warm,
blue wine, roselike waters of Venice.
I am told by many a cheap trick that Venice is too sweeeet!
this time of year.
The fragranced yellow snuff plants are slumbered snugly in my travel bag
I carry a sack of hot-colored gel pens to write
back home to my lovers with.
Off now I go boated to sea, my lips tight upon a bowl of fresh Peaco tea.
It's all about me now, so I curl brown fingers in wind-chimed fog and sail.

I'm told that Venice is the bomb between
the seasons of winter and spring.
Catatonic's this musty brown sea, and for once,
maybe—it moves just for me.
Now and four tomorrows ago, I loved man after man like a dignified
whore. It's about me now, but my phone beeped
and my grown boy said, "Come home."
Mama, it's my turn to breathe as you are
the green trees of my infinite gardens.

Above beanie-capped swirls of wet curls that
wipe sea smoke off thick brows
I think of him far along a fried Venice ocean
that reeks of molasses and roe.
"Come home," he said, "cradle me again on your fat bosom and
premounted hips." he whispered from under tolls
where red sharks with X-ray gills could hear.
"It is illegal," he said, "for the heart of a woman
to beat while she lives in life."
So my defeated nostrils inhaled the last whiff of
freedom of the greasy seas.

And as the waters slept, like Mr. van Winkle, my boat turned around.
Back home like Red Riding Hood, I headed,
broken and down like the Titanic.
Yeah, Venice is juicy about now, but with a twist of
formaldehyde in its gut.
If ever you see the likes of Rome, you have seen
eternal infinity as a culture.
It's as ironically dead as was Christ on his fourth day inside his tomb.
My go smells of home-sugared cobbler and
fizzy root beer & a risen Venice.

SCORCHED PETTICOATS

A shimmering Eden in the west wing of the Calcutta Octagon
still holds my love for you
As I watch the so-called eyes for only me rape the voluptuous
figures of Southern girls.
Now I press my New York beanie flat to my up north scalp
and roll down my red dickie
And, lo, with suction from my fraternizing ears,
I listen low for catcalls of the Philly train.
Bubbie, did you ever not know that I would lift my two-bit cloak
and leave you in Dixie?

Oh, Dixieland for whom confederates have perished
beneath the foul hanky of geeches,
When, oh, so hot are the pulsating rays of Asian summers
that Indians melt like squaws.
When your hooped-hipped ladies sway hot bellies
like the serpent GOD sent to the floor
I see your tongue sag like my breast to lap up their flesh
like the hot lusty rebel you are.
Oh, you southern gentleman, to whom I have handled
your heart like lava-eyes gooone!

To you have I given the winds from my breath
and my razorblade-cold stuffed arteries
And below your glazed oil lamps, you looked up at my
Damned Yankee eyes for love.
On the cashmere boundaries of a platter of jades and grapes,
I gave you my salty soul.
Screwed by shame, I watch your womanizing lips kiss bye
to my horses, camels, & mules.
Oh, Tar Heel, limit not your farewells in the shamrocks of
partiality and also kiss my Ass!

A shimmering Eden in the west wing of
the Calcutta Octagon still holds my love for you
Like ganders laying waterfalls that came down from
my eyes like the Berlin walls.
Now the splendor of the Philadelphian passions hog
my heart like Boston-taxed tea
And your perplexing eyes follow the white lady
at the station in front of me to my train
Bub, look past the scorched petticoats of the ladies to my right—
you just might see me go!

You Will not Taste the Rain

(A Dedication to Kingsley)

You thought or you knew on the splendid chords to my heart's labor
that a lady somewhat above the ground still feels you in blood.
Though the seconds do churn away like grated butter
between winter and spring,
they are replaced by white-haired partiality in
years of stifling reminiscing.

Now maybe there is a season for knowing you are of
no more on this sensitive earth,
And just maybe my cabin walls no longer weep for
the likes of your brother's ole home.
And maybe, just maybe, I still smell your fresh life in
hot pines of chandeliered orchards,
but the dirt-old notion that you wait for me on the
spraying reservoirs of Heaven is real.

Crumpled fingers pocketed, I walk your fertilized
grounds as incandescent dusk at dawn.
I know you guy, by your democratic smile below
Camelot of brining musk in the fall.
I know you by an elegant ray of misty-eyed sparrows
above you as high as holiness.
But more so by the sweet solitude of the petrified fowl
that mates with carnal swans.

Swans that umbrella a soul that sleeps below
the merchants of breezy seas missing me.
Their wings stretched tight across a wine-washed sky,
beholding nothing less than dew.
If ever I be as lady as you were man, may it sleet for forty nights
in the rain forest of hell.
Know you now there is no such thing as death,
just an intermission in the life that we live.

And next time before I crush you close to my flesh and sigh,
my heart will harbor love.
Next time below my buttered spoon,
my sashayed tongue will dip to interludes of death.
Next time before the seasons of the glaze-eyed ravens
that sing out your name,
I will mount you high as the icy pyramids of Everest,
and you will not taste the rain.

WHERE ARE THE CARTS

Last night inside popping store carts and cheap price tags, my family disappeared,
And me, let me enjoy the last residues of my grape juice, I told them, and I will later be in the store.
But as I no less than slammed shut the candy red of my fine Eddie Bauer, I thanked God for my perseverance, or so I thought. Sprayed and romantic pats of sweet southern rain washed the devil-stenched earth as my size seven shoes turned to her store or God's.
And I stooped and peered beneath the Mussolini drops that betrayed such a temperate and sentimental night.
Among this a most beautiful senior in and around the world whispered through the seductive trees.
My cremated ears rose like Lazarus for Jesus, and I heard this girl ask me, "Hey, John Hardin teacher, where are the carts?"
With my soul I smiled, and I spoke with that smile, "Those carts are in Heaven in the book of life, where they are destined to be.
And who may you be standing here looking like the dry leaf brought back to my ark after the flood.
You have that much and more courage for the brain cancer that you refused in this life to call your own."
Where are the carts? I heard you sigh in a frustration that died without ever once living?
I fingered and knawed at my head as white as Mary Picklesgill, and this so-called damned Yankee remembered back to the days of Philadelphia.
Days where I ate my hot cheese hoogies over slumping, dying men who gave up the ghost for pennies and an orange.
Days when morbid old gals danced on the church corners to lose their lives to fishers of men, called Lucifer.
Days when the love of my life, my church was an agnostic old dream for the atheist.

But through it all, I heard your blessed malignant vocals ask,
"Where are the carts to strength and grace, Teacher?"
And like the teacher that my God ravished upon me, I spoke,
"Your chariots are in your strength,
Lift your brave reins high to red skies, and guide them by the strength of our Lord."

ONE HUNDRED COOL ROSES

I slouched on Meechie's last male kiss
as our washed-up love would end in pain
the soft-fallen shoulders of the kingdom I'd miss
is nothing left here but the prelude to rain.

A million hot tulips I'd give for his heart
oh, nothing much less than my homage to kings
the castrated secrets that we kept after dark
is nothing left here but the insteps to dreams

His lark is now ashes and his cigarette is void
his cloak is now bundled and farewell's in his eyes
my word's a plugged nickel and my life is destroyed
there's nothing left here but a cascade of lies.

I beheld my Euripides, a last firm kiss
I know that our season's eccentric and vain
the heaven's now spraying a euphoric mist
it's nothing less here than the breastplate to rain

if ever once more inside death we should live
without the confounds of the infidel, lust
a hundred cool roses, I know I can give
if all that's left here is the preamble to trust.

The Twenty-fifth Hour of the Day

Matrimonial rings no whiter than gold seeps a perilous
beam to the heavens of the room
And I sit with you above seafood and rolling tea
on a drowsy day at the captain's place
a sculptured mist that gleams from your seasoned plate
highlights before me, the groom
And for the first and last time in our thousand years,
I behold a sadness in your face.

Gummed-mouthed soldiers and waiters with pressed
white collars pass you by in vain
Newport smoke and clapping brown plates
encase your holy head as the public strides
Life rides on in the sweetest essence as we sit
in the inner folds of the cremated rain
And for the last to the first time beyond the year of our God,
I feel the sadness in your eyes.

The communist wind around us breathe into our
receptive ears a passing breath of powers
And I watch your tongue rise beyond the glassy halos
of silver dinner fork on your lips.
You spoke my own heart when you said that
it's hard to get through twenty-four hours
with one you've come to love by legal laws
that cracks the backs of slaves without whips.

So we sat and we dined by the daylight of night
in the boredom below the captain's skies
feeling each other's pain in the twenty-fifth hour
of this conversational day at sea
No more would I pretend not to catch the hints
that you gave by voice and with eyes
whenever I knew that you were speaking to me.

I still smell the dusty gold of a ceremonial wedding band
that is shining by law on the bay
So never will you not know that this poet was feeling
the poetry of your warranted pain
As we dined over seafood and sweet water on one
twenty-fifth hour of every blessed day

White Chapels

I look upon the smooching and Hiram-dancing flesh
of your fresh cigar as it rises to God
And I get the justifiable pleasure to think of you
in an indecent but respectable manner.
Your soft and innocent eyes that beheld no manly sin
has reneged upon nothing
As they gaze and they stare upon this
Helen-of-Troy beauty outside of the nicotine fog.
My Lord, how this lady aches to snatch you to
the other side of that shivering sweet smog
Seductively crushing your strong romantic lips with a fury
of the London Whitechapel socialist.

I look up at the belly-dancing smoke of your cigar
fraternizing with the troposphere
And under your hypnotizing smoke rings,
I see roaming brown eyes who loves another
He loves another who loves many without reservation,
constitution, or humble surprise

I look upon the Hiram-dancing flesh
of your fresh cigarette as it rises to a kingdom
Like opium it circles your words,
"I think that I love a Spanish Lady they call Rosa-leeta."
Like a cuing Whore she heard you serenade
in a cloud of dew one day, and stole my heart

Now low I sit below your inclement logs
amid swirls of Black and Mild, saturated eyed.
I know that you're gone for good, and all
that we dreamed of in our youth has left
With Rosa-leeta's sporadic awe for what I was born to own
and who was born for me.
The carriage cabins of my heart has been vandalized
and confiscated for what?
And a jilted, hurt lady aches to snatch you
to the other side of that shivering sweet haze
But a thief has White-chapeled the vow
that we as kids made with our fornicating blood.

A Cake with a Voice

My lover brought home a spice cake today
The words saying "I love you" had withered away
The brine from the icing now matted and worn
And the box's satin ribbon was so tattered and torn.

The taint of the mildew had began to set in
Reduced for quick sale had been written in pen
Upon a ripped label that smelled like old tea
With a shabby burned candle he'd made just for me.

In all of the world there seemed no worst plight
Than this battlefield carcass I longed to delight
Much sweeter than fructose and as rayed as daylight
I romanced my wet tongue with the first warm bite.

My lover brought home a sweet cake today
The words saying "I love you" was chiseled away
But as cool whip will sour and icings may rub
The best taste in the world is from he whom you love.

THE SECOND STONE

(A song without music)

Jesus came out to Mount Olive one day,
and he stooped as he wrote in the sand.
He muffled his ears as to hear not the people
who asked that he stone this woman.
The sin of adultery, by the law of our Moses,
was clearly the blade on the knife.
No apologies taken or promises rendered,
for this she should pay with her life.

Chorus:
Yes, Jesus came out to Mount Olive one day,
and he stooped as he wrote in the sand.
He claimed not a word that the people were saying,
just wrote with an unwavering hand.
With time as a virtue and continuous pleaing,
he stood and he now faced the crowd.
The wisdom that poured from his lips was enlightening.
His message was quiet but loud.

"He who's among you that is without sin,
the first stone at her you will cast."
Again, he did stoop as he wrote with his fingers
and waited to witness this task.
In vain, Jesus waited for cracks of the stoning the sinless
would dare now to hold.
He stooped and he wrote in the sand as he noticed
that stone number one never showed.

Chorus:
Today, in my heart and at the edge of Mount Olive
I stand with stone two on God's land
just waiting to hear the first crack of the marble
that precedes the stone now in my hand.
I called and I wept and I yelled out with honor.
I stooped as I cried out in vain.
I waited in awe for so much of my life,
but the stone number one never came.

Chorus:
I know now the message that came from my Jesus,
I know why he spared us his rod,
for all man has sinned without purpose or passion
and come short of the glory of God.
I know now the message that came from Mount Olive
when Jesus did write in the sand.
No perfect of perfect could touch that poor woman.
There is no perfection in man.

Still Jesus came out to Mount Olive one day
and stooped as he wrote on earth's floor.
His plan for our lives we know is unchanging, to go and not sin anymore.
If ever you're out in Mount Olive one day, and
you stoop as you write in the sand,
remember the fate of the first casting stone
and never the one in your hand.

MY PASSIONS FOR CHRIST

With the utmost respect for the love of my God,
I came last night with vigor and honor.
Nothing in God's lamps beholding in me but the virtue
I held in the pulpit of raw sin.
Now I sat down below conservative chambers of
heaven's swellings to hear you speak.
Now I walked on the cold reservoirs of hypnotized seas for
echoes of a familiar genre.
Now I know it's not a song of lust when Mama too sang me
from the arms of my Buddha?
Were it not for the love of common kings
would I fancy so now my Passion for Christ?

Yet were it not now for the Passion of God,
I could not long for love of common kings?
Did you not know that the cracked cinders
of good sermon would romance me to GOD?
I live to feel God's holy embraces upon my feminine chest
resting in his padlocked arms.
My teacher has created this blazing love affair
with the love of both my lives.
Now by the unanimous mist of euphoriant air
around my canopy bed, I smell religion.
It is the oils of GOD's merciful kisses upon my lying tongue
for the passion of Christ.

Embracing like lovers, you said,
impeaching my every lust for just the hem of his garment.
You made me to lie with him, to gaze into his fiery eyes
'til my flesh blazed with holiness.
You made me want to stroke his strong,
wooly hair until I am baptized with righteousness.
You made me want to scream out his name
like the simultaneous orgasms in blessed sex.
You made me drop to my knees just holding God
in sacred places for the sake of worship.
Oh, minister called life, in brass rings and bracelets
you led me to the Passions of Christ.

THE SECOND MASTER

Tony thought to me I love you, as the second master
I've needed my true love to be.
I will hold you when your purse is fat
with the sweat of your liberated pen, my poet.
I will kiss your fine lips until the cold sun
drips black unicorn blood into the whipped sea.
And I will, like the world does best, hate you without a cause,
as you pray beneath God.

Never will I love you, you, and you and only you
by the grace of you, as the author of you.
My married heart lies with the cherubic ladies
below the Stetson hats and twisted minds.
Offer me youth and fostered beauty with skinny pockets they do,
unlike your yours aged,
And I will, like the world does best, hate you without a cause,
as you pray beneath God.

Through the aromatic wings of your unseeing love for me,
can you taste the tears of God?
If so, you have me forever and six years—
No love above love could mash a finger on this.
I curse me who longs to love you and only you by the grace of you,
as the author of you.
And I will, like the world does best, hate you without a cause,
as you pray beneath God.

As the years have been the Judas of your beauty and your verse,
unlike the young is raped,
I'll be one who bows down to strong tongue,
amniotic youth, and the virginity of ignorance.
I'd curse me, were I to love you and only you
by the grace of you, as the author of you.
Still, as the world, I will love you my second master,
kneeling below the pedestals of God.

Old Christmas

Our very own Christmas in the inner city ghetto
was the refractioned bomb.
Off our splintered milk crates that only pretended to be tables, we dined.
Had we the same foul wind that bullied the epileptic windows of the rich.
It shook and jimmied the security of the panes to make its name known.

Now Mama, in her soiled Peejays and matted hair,
covered the iced up walls.
With respect to the hurling bricks of T-T,
not a single window pane we had.
The world got high on fat chowder
and watched hiramed snow beyond glass.
A winter wonderland outside,
I thought I heard the suburbs call it by name.

Our land of wonder? Over six feet of
incoming snow that Dee had to shovel.
Still we got elaborate corn dogs
and a cup mayonnaise for Christmas supper.
Bren had to draw our only Christmas tree
on shaggy wood floors with nails.
And in the name of the only God, I got to draw the presents we yearned.

Hey pea, who, now who, could have laughed sweeter than us ladies four.
Yeah, that was Dee and little me with our greasy smiles
by Mama and Bren.
I cherished every frostbitten flake by holy flake
that swan dived into our flat.
It was our own Christmas,
even when this pedestaled snow became breakfast.

Our solo Christmas in the slums of the slums was the refractioned bomb.
One that blew with the bending of Christmas lights
upon a mythical water.
One no less than the nostalgic gray-haired souls
of Dee & me as we strolled.
Six feet above an earth that once was Mama and Bren
in search of our old Xmas.

Kings Like Enoch

Through eyes swollen and cradled as Billy sacks like
the fourth coming of my Christ.
I peered at him through the filthy
and christened-wet window panes of my palace wall.
A grumpy little man he be with his bony,
slumped shoulders humped over outdoor film.
With a noble exterior of grace, his calloused,
cracked fingers scooped trash like jade.
And residues of dirt poured from his proclamated hand
like the tears of God
As he, about his job, collected trash
from the emancipated gutter on cold nights.

Like the stillness of the rope that hung the devil,
I watched him work without self—pity.
In the punitive frost of my Insubordinate candlelight,
I caught a glimpse of his features.
His tired and ole eyes socketed in holes plastered
above a peeling nose and scraggly beard.
His frail lips were parched, pursed, aged,
and starched with yesterday's liquor stains.
From head to metatarsals he was, by nature,
an entrepreneur of trash collection & garbage.
No less than a barefoot, dirty-clothed poacher
with a snot rag across a grimy left shoulder.

Still an apparition of the next two years
that had already come last fall showed his name.
Lord, my Lord, he be a king!
The regal way that he scooped his scepter from the dust
And arched his proud and noble back high above his trash throne
as any given earl would
My pink & somber night light flicked a quiet
and pleasant refraction of a protruding chin,
And at this eleventh hour of the hour,
I beheld his kingdom within his streetside throne room.
The under tolls of heaven rolled like fresh roe
as he smiled & walked like Enoch

Times of Fall Marigolds

When caroling winds shift musicless songs of aging summer to your listening ears,
how faint you do hear the last exhales of perishing marigolds at fall-start.
The end red dews of christening wine fall hard from old berries like Custer,
as September gives way to the birth of a fresh new year of your life.

Old familiars fade from your world like the tingles of marmalade on pursed lips,
and all that you know you have ever been in your life, for the first time, you become.
Funny it is how the concept of wisdom is the daughter of time in a parentless world,
yet time does not exist! Instead are merely subliminal and limitless boundaries in infinity.

Boundaries that forward our strides toward this throne room of God that we call heaven,
boundaries that yearly sway us closer to white-haired wisdom of ancient peyote dreams,
carcinogenic boundaries that kill the twice dead with a deadly death before dying,
boundaries leaving us to wash our white bodies white with euphoric desire for pureness.

Now giving thanks for winds of September, with a breach of distrust for the aging of age,
may you honor with a cataclysmic celebration of honor, another infinite year of wisdom,
and now within peering throughout the boundaries of life that we know as time, you grow
Funny how the perishing of summer marigolds brings forth new life within life unlived.

WORK TO BE DONE IN A CITY OF GOLD

(In memory of my sister-in-law, Delores)

by Kevin and Lynette Calvert

Now that your glorious days are done
and your rapture's summoned you home,
go unto GOD, you who have been heavily laden,
and come upon an elusive rest.
There are glaciers of memories of you in our hearts,
memories high as Mount of Everest.
Memories that outsoak the blessed waters
of the rain forest as the northern heavens weep.
Oh, you Lady Knight in glimmering armor called Delores,
you sleep not in our Lord GOD.

Can you recall when Kevin, your Rocket Gibraltar,
would go by sister's place to hold you,
and you would teach me each year
with the philosophy of a captain on GOD's holy ship?
Remember when I, Lynette, your brother's wife
watched you at a distance from our Lord?
And you fed my weak spirit with the loaf of your words
and from the flask of your thoughts?
Oh, Delores, we'll miss you on the threshold of this world.
May we meet you in the next.

Your emancipated soul has a fine role
of strolling in heaven's sweet orchards with God.
Now that your sun's settled into the cool waters of your busy life,
all work here's done.
There's much more to be done in heaven,
a city where the red carpet is paved with gold.
Unlike like some of us, Delores, you CAN!
go home again and in your soul, you have.
It's been a pleasure having been your younger brother
and sister-in-law in this life.
May you eternally live unisoned with peace,
each day washing the earth with memories.

You Can! Go Home Again

I sit tonight beneath a scorching winter sun,
bearing no love for the bushels of foul horseflies
pinching at my dry flesh, and I bore myself to sleep.
Within this strong woman breast,
there is an uncasual lust to taste the kingdom of home.
Yeah, it's me with my poison soda pop
and soggy bowl of chips in Dixieland
as I sit up on a filthy rock with the job of being jobless
for the tenth year straight.
cause I ain't in the family. Got ah useless Ph.D.
in hand while masturbating in education.
I could build a continent with my unanswered résumés
and my two-job rejection notes.
Yeah, it's me cursing within my second hour of waiting
for my town's only taxicab to ride me three blocks down
the road by the grace of sympathy.
It is my sentimental water pools that cascade down
my nostalgic blue cheeks as I dodge
The gut-bursting stench of stale mold
and terminal diseases within a Southern blue air.
It's I who fight off the nauseating smell of fatal car wrecks and well-used
insulin needles in a redneck town, where the streets are paved with
roadkill, and that holds no city gain.
There is an element of pain for the damned
in this roach-egged home out of my North.
And I'll not share the calamity of hurt with the native blue Dixies.
I must go home again, where cool summer air cleanses my shamed soul
A home, where the Baltimore sun
complements the virginity of America in the raw.
And the aromatic perfumes of modern medicine spice
the air like the climax in sex.

Yes, it's me in my big office
and corporate easy chair who sits back and laugh,
toasting with my executives for a job well done
within a city well loved, without vanity.
It is I who suck the last of expensive Bay-imported seafood
rinsed by the piña colada.
as I climb into my waiting pool of professional limousines
retreating to my palace.
I see the images of hot party-lit city street fights
highlighting an anticonfederate notion.
This is the desire of this elusive pure heart.
My hot skin is steaming and my marathoned heart is racing
toward the city I do so adore.
Oh, captive of a Southern city that holds me in bondage as does pharaoh,
by the mercy of GOD and the way of a sea that is Red, do loosen your
crisp Southern whips—and let this lady go home again.

THE STORIES—FICTION AND REAL

All Men Are Rapists

All men are rapists, and you are the king of your kind.

These twisted words dripped from my young mouth like the sexual plague. I was speaking to my mom's cousin Harri-Lee as he sat in the emergency room at Pitts Church Hospital in Raleigh, North Carolina. It was a few days before Thanksgiving during the bicentennial year. I had just graduated from high school and enrolled in a local state university in Albany, New York. The university was a few hours away from my home in Northwest, Washington DC "*Shh*! Lynne," my new husband, Kevin, whispered to me.

"I never raped anyone, and never will," said my seventeen-year-old Army private husband, who had just finished basic training and AIT at Fort Knox, Kentucky.

"I know, Kevin, I am sorry," I whispered under my breath. "But when I was four, I watched my two sisters beat and brutally raped by my mother's first cousin, tomjack. They were only six and seven years old when it happened, and they ended up with syphilis afterward. After this, I resided among the worst types of men between Washington DC and Brooklyn, New York."

"I know," said Kevin, comforting me, "I was there too, we grew up together, remember?"

"How well I remembered quite a lot," I said as I glared at rev. herold lee king (harri-lee), my mother's Aunt Mamey-Leah's son from Raleigh.

To the right of my glare, a porker of an Indian doctor who appeared to be at least seven feet tall darted from one of the back rooms of the hospital and handed harri-lee a small piece of paper.

"Here is your prescription, rev," he said. "Be sure to apply them to the burns on your face every six hours, and do not use any bandages. If your symptoms persist after ten days on this stuff, make another appointment to see me again in my clinic."

"Sure thang, brother." Harri-lee nodded as he removed the prescription from the doctor's plump hand and stood up to leave.

I could not believe that Mama had sent Kevin and me to take Harri-lee to the hospital after his twenty-year-old sister, Rochelle Mylinda, had flung a pan of boiling hot fatback grease into his face. To me, this was the best gift that she could have given harri-lee after what he had done to her. I was so sorry that Mama had moved back to her late father's hometown of Raleigh after I graduated from high school up north. Mama and the rest of our immediate family had been born and raised up north.

I was now home from college on a Thanksgiving break, and Kevin was on leave before starting his first tour of duty in Germany. I would join him there after accumulating a few college credits. Kevin and I had decided to visit Mama for Thanksgiving. After all, she did make the best sweet potato pie and broiled turkey on the low side of the moon. Kevin and I had not counted on running into cousin harri-lee again. As of this day, he was now the new pastor of the biggest Baptist Church in Raleigh. Harri-Lee had been living and preaching in Chocowinity for about ten years now and had only been back in Raleigh for one day. He came back because, thanks to his mom, he had been selected to serve as pastor of the Baptist Church after the ex-pastor, old man Johnny Belles was diagnosed with Alzheimer's a few weeks back. Harri-lee had just rented the duplex that was attached to my mother's apartment in Raleigh. It was across the road from his mom, who was my mom's late father's sister, Mamey-Leah. In addition to harri-lee, Mamey-Leah had fifteen other adult children who lived with her or in the vicinity. Harri-lee's sister, Rochelle Mylinda, was the youngest of all the children. Harri-lee was smack in the middle of the sixteen children.

In any event, Kevin, harri-lee, and me got into Mama's white Bonneville and took off for Mama's house. The trip home from the hospital was filled with tensed emotion between Kevin, me, and harri-lee. Harri-lee was well aware that I hated him for what he had done to my cousin, Rochelle Mylinda, and this forty-five-year-old so-called minister had no love for me either.

Vrooomm, vrooomm! raged the antiquated Bonneville as it took off down the rural road with busting dust balls fogging up the indigent trail as if it were a national smokehouse. In the hems of silence, I clutched Kevin's right arm as he drove us back to Mama's place. Through the sideview mirror on my end of the car, I could see harri-lee drifting off to sleep as if he had the right to do so. With his burned face, he looked as if he had just experienced a fifteen-minute stay in the heart of the Chicago Fire. The fact that he was no looker before his burns did not help either. At that point, I could not hate harri-lee any worse, and my mind kept drifting off to all the events that led up to this hospital adventure.

Rochelle Mylinda King was ten years old and going to the fifth grade when her thirty-five-year-old brother, harri-lee, raped her.

It had been the second day of summer vacation, and all the children were bubbling with excitement. The summer vacation had finally rolled around. In any case, it was ten o'clock in the morning, and Rochelle Mylinda had decided to sleep in. Aunt Mamey-Leah and everyone else had gone to work on the tobacco truck, I guess, putting in tobacco for the local farmers. Rochelle Mylinda could not go because she was too young. Her brother Pookie, who was the second from the youngest, always watched her, but he had just started putting in tobacco also. "You have to be at least sixteen to do the job," Pookie had told her, and Pookie had turned sixteen a few days ago. Since Pookie was working now too, Aunt Mamey-Leah needed someone to watch her. This particular day, harri-lee, who never worked as anything but a pastor, volunteered for the job. The story that my elder cousin told me was that she and harri-lee, who lived at home with their mom at the time, were the only ones in the house that day. Everyone else was out working in tobacco. Ten-year-old Rochelle Mylinda shared a room with her sixteen-year-old niece Skeeta-Mae. Unfortunately, Skeeta-Mae too had gone to work in tobacco. The wee hours of the morning reflected an ever-so-soft ambiance of serene tranquility as the rim-sleeped Rochelle Mylinda glanced up misty-eyed at the ghost tiptoeing into her bedroom. This slow apparition would turn out to be none other than her brother, harri-lee. Unafraid of her tobacco-chewing, snuff-dipping, alcoholic brother, harri-lee, she turned her face to the wall and attempted to go back to sleep when harri-lee staggered into her room stinking like a relieved polecat in a cheap bootleg steel. Sleepily, Rochelle Mylinda peeped around once more to notice the usual dumb-looking grin on harri-lee's ugly face as he commenced sneaking into her room like the Grinch who stole Christmas. She peered at his wine-stained lips and hooked nose as he pulled the covers from her small thighs and lay down behind her in the bed. He then pushed her all the way back around to fully face the wall. It was then that she felt a stiff and hard, meaty oblong object sliding back and forth between her thighs for what seemed like hours upon days. Feeling like a concentration camp Jew just visited by Adolf Hitler, she began to cry. The more she cried, the harder her Hitler thrusted while involuntarily choking her until she felt her already asthma-infected throat shriek with pain. Rochelle Mylinda cried out violently for help with her unheard pleas for mercy as she wildly fought the air for her freedom. She had not the strength to loosen herself from this poltergeist called Samson. He was just too strong. Still, she gagged and screamed for her mom. Her young world, until now, had always consisted of the tasty raisin cookies that our aunt Tillee always baked, cardboard paper dolls, and her mother's soft bosom. Now her bugging eyes, under excruciating pain, had no clue how to accept whatever was happening to her.

The endless minutes that harri-lee molested and brutalized his child sister seemed like years until his ecstatic, smelly, male body began to shake and heave in a frenzy; and he saturated the child's vaginal area with a hot, sticky, and foreign wetness. He then pushed her little head painfully and violently into the wall that she faced, rose up from the bed, and left the room, leaving behind his offensive stench.

"Elf you tell iny body," he yelled to his shocked, now-fearful, young sister over his shoulder, "Ima kill you and them too."

After harri-lee left the room, the perplexed, shaking, and scared Rochelle Mylinda waited a few minutes and listened to him ease out of the back door like a thief. It was then that she ran next door to the neighbors' homes, banging frantically on the doors, scared beyond comprehension. Ms. Ertha yelled, "You liar! Your brother is a preacher and the pastor of my church. He wouldn't do that." Miss Nee-Nee said the same thing, and so did Deacon Bobby Ray from their church. Rochelle Mylinda screamed to the top of her lungs, running up and down the streets until someone finally managed to locate her mom by telephone. Aunt Mamey-Leah was home so fast that one would be inclined to believe that she had rode home in a race car. It was then that she grabbed Rochelle Mylinda by the shoulders, looked at her, and informed her that harri-lee would never do such a thing. She further refused to let the sulking, all-alone child call the police on her son. Rochelle Mylinda was all alone now.

That night after service, harri-lee had the audacity to flaunt his foul-smelling carcass at his mother's house as if nothing had happened. He sat down to the dinner table, removed a big reeking ball of Apple Tobacco from his right cheek, and gulped down the collard greens, rice, and pig tails that his mom had cooked. There was an unusual, haunted silence about the dinner table that night as everyone ate without speaking. As harri-lee finished freeloading at his mom's dinner table, he stood up with the dignified back arch of a blatant homosexual, stuffed a gigantic row of Scotch snuff in his bottom lip, and left the dinner table with his Bible tucked under his right arm. Off he went, on the way to prepare his next sermon. At this point, the friendless Rochelle Mylinda somehow found the strength to yell to him, "Ms. Nee-Nee said that you are not a rapist, but you are. **All men are rapists**, and if it takes me the rest of my life, I will get you back for what you did to me!" There was a chain gang silence at the table as everyone preoccupied themselves with working on their meals.

The seconds finally metamorphosed into a decade, and during the year of the bicentennial, my cousin Rochelle Mylinda, who had not spoken to harri-lee in the ten years since the incident happened, carried out her threat to her brother. A few weeks after the incident had happened, harri-lee was dismissed as pastor of a local church, and Deacon Bobby Ray took his spot. Harri-lee had been dismissed for sexual misconduct with a minor; the teenage son of one of the local wealthy businessmen had made a claim that harri-lee had paid him two dollars for sexual favors in the pulpit one night when he volunteered to stay and help harri-lee clean after the church gathering. After this claim was made, harri-lee was sent away from the church, but no one ever did believe Rochelle Mylinda's story. After being expelled from the church, harri-lee fled to Chocowinity. This day, ten years later, was harri-lee's first day back home, and he had been hired as pastor of a different church. Although I had not been visiting North Carolina when my cousin Rochelle Mylinda was attacked by harri-lee, she had told me about it over the phone. My mom, Kevin, and I were the only ones who believed Rochelle Mylinda though.

In any event, today harri-lee had come back to Raleigh for some of his mom's home-cooking on Thanksgiving and the new job that she had gotten him. Instead, harri-lee found twenty-year-old Rochelle Mylinda in the kitchen, boiling fried fatback in a huge pan of pissed-off grease. The instant that harri-lee walked into the kitchen and attempted to greet her, she yelled, "All Men Are Rapist!" and violently flung the pan of scalding hot grease directly in harri-lee's face! This was her first communication with harri-lee in ten years. Although harri-lee suffered from second—and third-degree burns, he refused to press charges against Rochelle Mylinda as the doctor that treated him had suggested.

After all, he admitted to Mama that night, "I did rape her like she said when she was just a child."

I glanced again through my sideview mirror at the snoring old man called harri-lee who was asleep in the backseat of the car. To me, he looked better with his face all blistered up and cooked like a pot of cabbage than he did before the hot-grease episode. Looking at harri-lee, I finally came to a realization. Because of tomjack raping my sisters when I was just four years old, because of harri-lee raping his ten-year-old sister, because my drunken aunt Poochie Pie was grabbed from an alley behind a local bar and repeatedly raped and beat up by a strange man with a jackknife when I was six, and because after I turned eleven years old, my mother's ex-boyfriend's adult brother always winked at me when no one was looking, I had formed first impressions of all men just like Rochelle Mylinda had. Because you only get one shot at first impressions, I had somehow formed the opinion during my critical years that all men were rapists. Little did I know at the time that no true man had ever raped anyone. It was only replicas of men that would even consider such gross and violent acts. It was then that I had realized that these beautiful men were God's gift to earth, and certainly not all of them were rapists.

The last time that I saw Rochelle Mylinda around harri-lee was not too long ago. I was in my late forties. Kevin and I had taken our three grown children and our three younger children and gone to Raleigh to visit my mother's grave. Mama had died on her third heart attack shortly after I had turned twenty-five. The chain-smoking Pookie had just died of lung cancer and had been buried beside my mother and her mother who had died of old age. After we put flowers on all three graves, Kevin suddenly turned around to a startling discovery. It was Rochelle Mylinda standing and staring down at a run-down tombstone that read, "Preacher-man harri lee."

Beneath his name, someone had taken a sharp object and scratched a lie on his tombstone that read, "All men are Rapists!" What I saw next sent warm and dancing vibes through my cool flesh. Rochelle Mylinda rubbed her graying right temple and instinctively bent down toward the weather-beaten tombstone, and with a sharp rock, scratched out the words "All men are" and replaced it with the words "was a." It now read, "Preacher-man harri-lee was a rapist!"

Caught, Like Butterfish

"This story is only for the stupid or mentally ill. If you read it, then you are no better than they."

"What story, Uncle Duke?" answered Beverly's brother Tutts. Beverly and Tutts stared at the make-believe book that their Uncle Duke pretended to hold up as he spoke the words, "This story is only for the stupid or mentally ill. If you read it, then you are no better than they."

"That's just it," said Uncle Duke, "the reason that I am not holding up anything for real is because there are no such stories." Uncle Duke scratched his graying fortyish left temple, and smiled the only smile that seemed to melt women and children like a chocolate bar on top of a California July sun. Tutts knew instantly that Uncle Duke was referring to that mean ole Tom Stone in Tutts's second-grade class. Uncle Duke had walked into Tutts's classroom today when Tom Stone was calling Tutts's creative story retarded just after Tutts had finished reading it during creative story time in Ms. Lanay's class. The story was about Tutts's Uncle Duke. The same Uncle Duke who had taken into his home Tutts's mom, Tutts's five-year-old sister Beverly who was in the kindergarten and suffered from developmental verbal apraxia and a moderate-severe delay, and himself. "Uncle Douglass Kade (Duke)," read Tutts earlier, "is a famous politician who is a Christian Republican in East Orange, New Jersey, where they lived." Uncle Duke also owned their beautiful big home with the private suites for every family member and an in-ground swimming pool. It was so nice of Uncle Duke to take in his younger sister and her two children, Tutts and Beverly, when their father had disappeared like a poltergeist just before Beverly was born. Tutts loved the fact that Uncle Duke was rich, overly popular, and kind to everyone. Still, it was just something behind Uncle Duke's eyes that Tutts could not quite explain. One day, he expected to find out what it was. What Tutts did not care to find out was just how popular Uncle Duke was, with or without those eyes. As Tutts's thoughts exited the revisited earth like a meteorite, he noticed Uncle Duke taking Beverly by the hand while nodding at all the passing vehicles that were hissing their horns and waving at him as if he were the Paul Newman of the suburbs. "It's time for you guys to get into the house. It is cold out in this driveway, plus it is getting dark," said Uncle Duke.

Tutts loved when Uncle Duke babysat them while his mom worked at the Red Cross on the weekends. Uncle Duke would always send Shameka, the housekeeper, and Mr. Jimmy, the cook home early, and instead of dinner, they got to eat good snacks and stay up late. Still, Uncle Duke always took Beverly to the suite that she shared with their mom and rocked her to sleep. Beverly got personal butler service from Uncle Duke. Beverly had to go to bed early because she was the youngest. Tonight was no different.

Soon after the potato chip, fruit roll-up party dinner, Tutts grabbed two grownup movies from the lazy wooden entertainment center in the living room and fled to his own suite, on the second floor of their four-story home.

Aaaaah, alone at last, he thought, lifting his head toward the kidnapped sun and the fourth floor where Beverly and Uncle Duke were. It was so beautiful how quiet the house was without Ms. Shameka, the maid, fussing and yelling something about those dumb cashmere carpets in the house and the so-called wipe-your-feet speech. Why couldn't she be as unparticular as Uncle Duke? The evening sky was now all the way blueberry with a hint of pearlized plums for clouds. Before settling neatly beneath his powder-blue satin comforter and sheets lying neatly across his king-sized bed, Tutts popped in a DVD titled *Kiss my Cookies*. Somehow in the air, there was a rather chilling and unusual sensation to check on Beverly, but Tutts knew that good ole Uncle Duke never liked being disturbed when he rocked Beverly to sleep. Tutts had gotten in trouble before for going up to the next floor and knocking on the door while Uncle Duke was in the locked room with Beverly, trying to get her asleep. For this reason, Tutts scrapped the whole idea of intruding and began drifting off into dreamworld. After all, the next day was Saturday. This was the day that Uncle Duke had promised to take him and his friends to the country ship hole to catch butterfish. Tutts just loved to watch how, when butterfish were pulled from the waters, they always looked extremely caught. They would lower their oval heads back toward the ocean and drip four single drops of tears back into the water. Uncle Duke always told them that by crying, these butterfish were paying homage to the waters that they would never see again. How well Uncle Duke remembered the culture of the butterfish. *Butterfish . . . fish, fish, fish, fish, fish,* Tutts kept thinking, but his dreams suggested otherwise.

Now there was a heightened and fragranced silence that fell over their serene home in the holiness of the so-called infant night. *Cogggggggg, shoooooooooh, coggggggggg,* sure snored Tutts, fast asleep. Somehow out of nowhere, Tutts's dreams kept abandoning the butterfish and taking him back to last week's sit-in on Dr. Deborah Vines's classroom. This was Beverly's teacher whom Tutts dearly loved. In his dream, Tutts remembered the new private zones curriculum that his school had started using with children who thought only a little bit good like Beverly. He dreamed sweet dreams of the private zones curriculum and how it taught the older siblings to watch for signs of sexual abuse in their younger sisters or brothers who had special or no special needs and to act as detectives. Tutts loved the idea of how he had signed up for the eyes and ears program of private zones. This program taught other sisters and brothers to watch and also listen for sexual abuse signs that their mentally disabled sisters and brothers were not able to watch for because of their disabilities. Tutts also felt content that he himself did not have anything to worry about where Beverly was concerned. She was safe because she was with Uncle Duke tonight. Nothing could possibly go wrong here. Uncle Duke was not only her uncle, he was the well-respected and popular uncle that men, women, children, and animals loved, respected, and adored. Tutts knew that they all were safe whenever Uncle Duke was near. Uncle Duke had once fussed about their next-door neighbor, Mr. Davon, the doctor, for just being alone with Beverly when his wife was babysitting Beverly and him. Uncle Duke was everybody's good ole Uncle Duke. Even Tutts's friends called him "Uncle Duke." Uncle Douglass Kade was not only a Christian and a deacon in church, but he also kept the rest of the family in the word of GOD as well. Tutts slumbered and dreamed how he loved his Uncle Duke dearly, but he loved Beverly even more. So why was he not seeing the situation for what it looked like? As a new deputy in the eyes and ears program, Tutts knew that eventually he would. He would . . . he would . . . he wooooooo . . .

Silence painted itself the color gold and Tutts could finally, actually hear a sweet, soft voice calling his name.

"Get up, wake up Tutts," the fine voice of his mom interrupted this gold as if that gold belonged to a fool instead of being at the end of Tutts's rainbow.

"Thank you," said Tutts and Beverly's mom with tears in her soft gray eyes.

"I would have never, ever guessed? . . . How could you ever have known?" sobbed Mom.

"You brave little man," said Mom, squeezing both her children tightly.

With his cherubic little face pressed against the embroidered red cross on Mom's uniform, Tutts began to drift back into this life. He began to remember what he had, in his sleep, decided to forget.

In his dream, Tutts could just not stop dreaming of butterfish caught and crying in a slimy sea-weeded net as he went fishing with Dr. Vines and the members of sibling detectives from the eyes and ears program of private zones.

Kissing Mom's red cross, Tutts began to snicker. Mom had always accused him of sleepwalking, this time she was right.

Tutts hazily peered through the molecular structure of the magic fog that only pretended to fill the room as the tension and shame among the room dwellers grew. Within this haze, Tutts spotted at the door a fat red-faced police officer who was missing a neck and had a giant Easter egg for a belly.

The egg-belly cop pulled out a busted walkie-talkie—looking radio and kissed it.

"Yeah, we gott-em," he spoke closely into the radio as he attempted to wipe sweat from the back of his neckless shoulders with a pudgy free hand.

"Well," spoke Officer No-Neck into his toy walkie-talkie, "apparently, the little boy got outta bed, and Momma claimed him to be sleepwalking." The officer snickered. "Yeah, he called the perpetrator Dr. Davon," he said cynically and with a smirk on his round face.

"The little boy went upstairs to the room of the victim, who is also his little sister. The little sister's name is Beverly and she is retarded—"

"Delayed!'" corrected Mom sharply.

"Sorry," lied the officer, continuing his story.

"Inyway," said Neckless, "the boy, Tutts, is a deputy in that new private zones program they using at the elementary schools now. The program teaches siblings of special needs kids how to recognize the signs of sexual abuse in retard . . . I mean, delayed"—egg-belly corrected himself, glancing over at Tutts's mom—"individuals who cannot speak for themselves. Iny ways, little Tutts implemented the blue-tag game of private zones. This is when the eyes and ears deputy has Mom to pour a secret transparent powder on private places on the child with special needs during bath time. This powder will last for either forty-eight hours or until the next bath time. Tutts had Momma to put some on Beverly this morning when Momma bathed her before school. Inyways, five minutes after the application of this powder, every time that the child is touched bare for at least forty seconds in the area where the powder was applied, the part of the perpetrator's body that touched the child in that area, will turn blue. This bluing cannot be removed, but it will wear off in seventy-two hours." Officer Neckless laughed. "Clever, huh, lets us know whooz during what."

"Inyways," continued the fat cop, "Tutts caught his Dr. Davon this way."

"Excuse me, Mr. Officer," interrupted Tutts's mother to Egg-belly, "you got the names wrong. The perpetrator was not Dr. Davon, it was my brother Douglass." She pointed across the room to the handcuffed Uncle Duke. "Tutts just got mixed up with the names because he was half-asleep when he contacted help."

Tutts and his uncle had a pact. Uncle Duke and Tutts promised each other that neither of them would go to bed at night without a handshake on the weekends. "Inyways," continued the porker through his radio, "fortunately, Uncle Duke was so anxious to get little Beverly alone that he forgot Tutts's usual weekend handshake tonight. Luckily, Tutts had not forgotten. He got up out of his bed, climbed the stairs to Beverly's suite, and banged on the door, demanding his handshake. I guess not wanting to make anything look suspicious, Uncle Duke slowly opened the door to the dark room and stuck out a blue hand to give Tutts a shake. Because the room was dark, I guess Uncle Duke did not know that his hand had turned blue. Still, Uncle Duke had not been informed about private zones. Like the good soldier, this seven-year-old boy, Tutts, shook his uncle's hand casually, and unconcerned, walked away quietly as his uncle closed and relocked the bedroom door where he and Beverly were. Still dazzled, Tutts then proceeded back down to his suite and commenced calling the emergency unit of Dr. Deborah Vines's child molestation swat team. Unfortunately, Tutts was so sleepy that he dialed the wrong number. He accidentally called the maid, Ms. Tomeeka—"

"Hold it!" shouted the husky female voice of Ms. Shameka, through the static of the broken police radio.

Tutts looked up to see Ms. Shameka's pretty dark face. She stood—big-boned—with her fist on her thick hips in front of the egg-gut officer.

"First of all," retorted Ms. Shameka, "I am not a maid, but a cleaning technician, and my name is not Tomeeka. I am Miss Shameka. Lastly, git your big feet offa that white rug I jest cleaned this afternoon. Don't be coming up in here messing up now cause you is the police. You feeling this?" asked Ms. Shameka boldly.

"Yes, ma'am," said the fat egg-stomached officer with the startled look on his face as he leaped off Tutts's cashmere throw rug and onto the shellacked walnut-finished floor. Abandoning his radio conversation and walking over to the two tall thin pinched-nosed police officers who looked like twins, he yelled, "Get that child-molesting pig outta here and lock him up!"

"Wha . . . ?" protested the pinch-nosed on the right of Uncle Duke, bending his head to look beneath the dropped head of Uncle Duke. "We can't do this, not only is this man really prominent in this community, but he is a Republican in addition to being a deacon in my church."

"I don't care if he is the duke of Tambodia!" shouted officer. "What's his gut, he molested this special needs child, and he is going to jail. I got here first, didn't I? When Tutts called Ms. Shameka, she was nice enough to drive to the station and have me come back with her to this house. Unfortunately for Mr. Duke here," said Egg-belly, nodding in distaste toward Uncle Duke, "he was still in the room with her. Billy and me tipped up the stairs and silently picked the lock. We caught this guy fondling this naked child with blue hands."

"Now if that ain't molestation, nothing is! I am in charge here, not you, and I say lock him up now!" yelled Mr. No-neck.

All of this was happening so fast, Tutts could not believe it was even possible. What had Beverly done so wrong to Uncle Duke to make him treat her like this?

Looking around his room or Grand Central Station, Tutts saw Mr. Jimmy stick his long skinny neck through the doorway of Tutts's room and yell to Uncle Duke, "I knew you were doing unnatural things to that little girl, I could tell by the way you always wanted to be alone with her all the time. You a pig! You ain't no better than that daddy of mine! Yeah, that's right, he molest me too when I was jest thirteen. I know the signs. An you better gimme my check before you go to the slaughterhouse!" Mr. Jimmy was pushed back out of Uncle Duke's face by the pinch nosed officer.

"I ain't never liked you no way, Mr. Uppity who got caught," yelled Mr. Jimmy through Mama's sobbing and loud crying.

"I can't believe it's my own brother! My big brother," cried Mama.

Then Mama's eyes went big as she dropped her head and quietly whispered, "I was in denial with my children. When I was little, Duke touched me too."

There was then a brief mourning silence in the room. In fact, it was so silent that Tutts had to look around for the pallbearers. At this, Ms. Shameka walked over and held Mama tight. Tutts was surprised at how tight Ms. Shameka seemed to have held his mom. Had she been molested too?

There was so much commotion in the room that Tutts almost didn't hear his fabulous Uncle Duke whisper to his sister, "Daddy touched me too."

Almost everyone was crying now except the officers. From this, Tutts could see that his little sister was not the only victim, they all were.

As the pinched-nose on the left of Uncle Duke began mumbling something about what Uncle Duke had the right to do, two more unknown officers rushed into the room, slammed his honorable uncle up against the wall like a slab of lunch meat slapped on a slice of bread, kicked his legs apart, and patted him down like the criminal that he was. They then escorted him out. The neckless officer grabbed up Tutts's DVDs and said over the radio, "Both kids here have been molested, the little boy was allowed to watch an adult-rated DVD and a pornography DVD titled *Kiss my Cookies*."

On the way out, Tutts could not believe what he saw as he and Uncle Duke's eyes met and locked for the last time. Four dirty tears dripped from Uncle Duke's eyes as if he was paying homage to the floors. Thanks to private zones, Uncle Duke was caught, like butterfish.

Chicago Fires

The days that I cherish best are those of my youth back in Manhattan, New York.

We lived in the Old West Death Valley area located just behind the New York Theatre on Broadway and Forty-second Street. I was sixteen, Abuu and Fatima were seventeen and fraternal twins, and Twwolla (Toe) was twenty. Abuu, Fatima, and Toe were native Nigerians who had migrated to East Orange, New Jersey, two years earlier with their father. Their mother lived next door to my family in Executive Alley just beside the White House in Washington DC. I lived in DC as well but spent my summers in Manhattan with my mother's sister, or my artist-dad in Newark, New Jersey. Each day, Abuu, Fatima, and Toe caught the path from East Orange to Manhattan to see me and to sell shish kebabs on the corner with their father. Their father paid me ten dollars per week for helping them.

Along about four o'clock each day, the four of us would finish up and enter our little man-made Death Valley village that rested in the most tranquil molehill of peace and serenity that ever rained upon God's earth. It was not heaven for us, it was a parade on a feather pillow without band, song, voice, or harmony. It was rest. Yes, it was here that we laid our heavy-laden bodies and rested. This was where we went to escape the wild and fast-paced corporation of city life at the end of each day. Every day for two hours after work, the father of would visit his Haitian friends at the local bars to party and smoke purple haze. When he finished this socializing, he would call the day by its name, take his children, and go home. I would return two doors past the theatre, next door to Death Valley, to my home, carrying my head but not my heart. My heart stayed back in Death Valley with Toe. I had loved Toe in silence for the last two years, and for two years, he loved a black twenty-two-year-old prostitute named Ijuah. Ijuah originally lived in Brooklyn, New York, near my father's family but spent the majority of her time in Manhattan with us or in Harlem, New York. When she was in Manhattan, she was always invading our little Death Valley episodes, trying to be close to Toe. I hated Ijuah with fury. She was everything that I was not. She was fat with a bald head and a receding hairline. She also had bucked teeth. This was not to mention the fact that her breath always smelled like the I. W. Harper Whiskey that my father would drink after singing and performing in the twenty-four-hour nightclubs. Ijuah also stank of molded crawdads from the Chesapeake Bay. She hung out at the two-day parties at the Unhooked Generation and popped Doogie Bells and Peanut Butter with the local Banana Republic singers from the Ritz club.

Since age twelve, I had my pick of boyfriends. Although I could never see it, I was said to be quite pretty, unlike Fatima. I was also the best dressed and most polite of all my friends. I had turned down the most prominent guys by age sixteen. All these, to find my one true love. I found him in an ordinary Joe named Toe.

I always kept a keen sense of pride in myself. While my elder sisters turned two-dollar tricks on Fourteenth Street in DC, I was a proud female who bowed to no man. Fatima used to always tell me, "Lynne, the day is going to come when some man is going to break your heart into a million pieces as you break the hearts of so many others."

Fatima was a one-woman-girl. At seventeen, she had been with the same lover for the last two years. She was engaged to an eighteen-year-old girl named Linda, whom she married in Baltimore two years later. I too wanted to commit to someone, but that someone had to be the best man between Neptune and Troy. I was so desired that young boys would lie about having affairs with me. Still, my love belonged to Toe. Abuu used to tease me about being in love with his elder brother. Still, I was well aware that he himself was having a sexual affair with an older man named Mr. Chester that owned the gay bar on the corner. They had met at one of the usual four-day Manhattan orgies and hit it off ever since. In any case, I stuck to my books and my pride and worked hard to become my mother's cashmere dream. Her heart's desire was for me to keep peace with the world and become the poet and writer that she once had been. So being the Richard Corey (without putting a bullet through my head) that I was, I too cursed the bread and struggled to be the educated lady that Mother wanted me to be.

Still, every afternoon in Death Valley, I had the chance to be whomever I pleased.

On the days that Toe's beloved Ijuah was not present, I enjoyed being with the twins and Toe. I wanted so much for Toe to notice me, but Mama's teachings would always sink in. I had to be a real woman at all times. A real woman was not allowed to approach a man by any means. I could not call a man on the phone, request a date, or defile my body with him in any way, for as Mama always said, "My body is the temple of the Lord." This was the culture of my upbringing in yesterdays and all my todays.

Still, I can never forget that day that Toe, Fatima, Abuu, and myself sat in Death Valley on my Goose Feather European quilt listening to 1970 45s that my father brought hot from the local corner thieves. Because we could see what appeared to be the entire New York from the Mount Everest of the small hills where we sat close, it seemed as though neither London nor China was beyond our reach from this holy spectrum. Just five minutes earlier, we had witnessed Toe's father robbing an old man at gunpoint, beating him, and then taking his hard-earned social security check, and running while the beat street police officers ate their corned beef sandwiches and cheered him on. Afterward we laughed at the finale of the robbery when the New York police officers did what they did best and stole the old man's hubcaps from his car. Today, nothing really fazed us. Toe, who mainly talked to his brother up at Death Valley, never said more than ten words in two hours to me, yet he was very attracted to other ladies. In addition to this, other men except him, were quite attracted to me. This was sad because like a well-smoked cigarette, I would have mashed beneath my feet all the Jimmies of the globe just to hold his precious hands. Yet still, I knew that I had to keep faith with my respectability, so I like Saint Nick, spoke not a word, but went straight to my work. In this case, my work was getting Toe to notice me. I had no clue how, so I just changed the record. It was then that I put on a record that was made by mother and her sister. My mother had been a singer like my father.

"Is that your mother?" said Toe suddenly to me.

I was shocked that he was speaking to me.

"Yeah," I laughed shyly as I kind of lowered my head in ironic embarrassment.

"I did not know she sang Christian music," said Toe. "I heard her sing when we first arrived in DC. She has a great voice just like your dad."

"I taught them everything that they know," I said jokingly to Toe.

It was at this point that my world became that rare and sensitive pearl that slept in elusiveness on the carpets of my oyster because for the first time, his deep brown eyes stared into mine as he laughed at my joke.

For the first time, he looked at me and actually saw me as he looked at me. Not only this, he held this stare and our eyes locked as if they were in jail. My middle chest felt like it weighed over a million pounds right then. My heart felt like a massive heart attack with five clogged valves. A mouth-twisting stroke on my part probably could not have gotten my attention right then. This was my time, and I was not going to let any demon cruising hell screw it up. I say this because at this precise moment, I saw Ijuah approaching the Death Valley entrance. She was grinning like a Cheshire cat and scissoring her thick black, ashy legs up to interrupt my most sacred moment. Yeah, but this Northern lady was as prepared as the next "Damn Yankee." I had paid Toe-jam, one of the glue-sniffing junkies that hung out on the corners and smoked Crazie Ladies and Window Panes, to snuff out Ijuah. I had brought him a bottle of Quickie and given him fifty cents to grab Ijuah when he saw her and stab her, then take her around back and rape her. Even Ugly Toe-jam had to pass on the rape part. I was well aware that on August 6, 1945, an American plane dropped a single nuclear bomb on the Japanese city of Hiroshima. The explosion utterly destroyed more than four square miles of the city center. About ninety thousand people were killed immediately; another forty thousand were injured, many of whom died in protracted agony from radiation sickness. Three days later, a second atomic strike on the city of Nagasaki killed some thirty-seven thousand people and injured another forty-three thousand. Together, the two bombs eventually killed an estimated two hundred thousand Japanese civilians. Toe-jam looked worst than all the victims of these holocausts put together.

Still, "She too ugly to rape," Toe-jam said.

Still, because I made sure that Toe and the twins faced me while I faced the entrance below, they were unable to see what was going on down there. As Ijuah, went to run up to meet Toe, Toe-jam leaped out of nowhere like Houdini and grabbed her by her neck. Her neck was as thick as a professional football player, but Toe-jam got the job done. After grabbing her, he took out the machete that I stole from my father's war box and stabbed her twice in her left side. The trick was not to let her into Death Valley to be near Toe. Anyway, Toe-jam was able to cover Ijuah's mouth before she screamed. Right after this, I watched Toe-jam's friend, Sausage, appear out of nowhere like a ghost and slash her hand with the 1955 straight razor that I had stolen from the pawnshop and given to him in case he wanted to rob Ijuah. I watched Sausage snatch her purse and take the nickel bags of drugs and hypodermic needles that Ijuah had been making seven—and eight-year-old boys sell on the streets for her. Next, Toe-jam went through her pockets before she fell limp to the ground and stole a fistful of drug and pimp money. Toe-jam then threw the cheap blanket that I had given him over her, so no one would know who was under it. As Northern inner city dwellers, we were quite used to stepping over dead and/or half-dead bodies without concern or emotion. After the junkies fled, I was able to continue my little love session. I was intrigued as Toe took my face in both hands and said sarcastically, "Lady, what are you looking at down there, you look as if you seen someone get stabbed or something."

"Oh no, nothing like that," I lied.

It was then that my cosmic universe beamed and exploded like a sexual climax because Toe leaned down, put his firm lips against my soft lips, and passionately kissed me. I felt like I was the one walking on the water and sinking, not Peter. Only I did not look down. I sucked Toe's darting tongue in my mouth like a hungry baby as it circled and pulled in my own tongue. Toe's and my own tongue dripped saturated with our married spit. His tongue felt like it was a thousand feet long up against my tonsils as we kissed with the ferocity of the 1871 Great Chicago Fire. This kiss got so deep that when we came up to remember that we were counting on breathing, the twins had disappeared somewhere inside the caves of Death Valley to leave us privacy, I assumed. We kissed over and over again for at least an hour.

Before it was time to go, I knew that I had fallen in love with Toe. I never knew if Toe loved me back because we, for some unknown reason, never went back to Death Valley again. Toe and me talked on the telephone a lot after that, and he always referred back to this fiery kiss, but we never kissed or saw each other again. Toe married and divorced the unsuspecting Ijuah one year after she was released from the hospital from the stabbing. They were married for six months before Toe took their infant son and moved back to Nigeria with his dad. Fatima married Linda and moved back to DC. Abuu did the obvious, changed his sex, and later on became a prominent New York physician, living and practicing in the Bronx. This was after having three sons by Katie, his ex-wife. As the days bloomed and metamorphosed into decades, just after high school, I married a young DC guy who was in the tenth grade at the time and had grown up with our family. He lived just down from my family in Capital Heights, Maryland.

Still, I was never satisfied. My heart always searched for the man who could make me forget the flameless fire in Toe's kiss. I found him in 2006. It was the sweetest and most painful kiss that I have ever had in my entire life. My knight is named Tony. We had one night of inflamed passion that made the electric work of Ben Franklin look like mere firecrackers—so much for the Chicago fire. I only think of Tony when I breathe or hold my breath, no other time though. Every time that I look at him, I am able to forget Toe's kiss in Manhattan. No one else can make it happen. I then melt like refined sugar in a rain forest every second that I think of Tony sitting like the noblest of earls on the pedestals of my heart. I felt not Tony's tongue on the back of my tonsils, I felt it at the floors of my cervical vertebrae. I would tie my life to a hobo stick and take a journey through a million blazing hellfires, side by side with Lazarus just to hold my Tony.

I loved Tony from the warmth of Mama's birth canal, and I will love him as I listen to the cracking and bursting of earth grains that drip upon my casket as the undertaker's rusty shovel throws the last residues of life six feet above me—when my eyes grow too heavy to remember this world.

But like Mama said, "A lady must be a lady at all times." As I was born a woman with honor and respect, so shall I die! Tony held me and left me without feelings for me, worst than Toe, and now I must learn to reteach my shattered heart to beat again. Toe, I no longer remember. Tony, I no longer forget. After all, Tony loves another who only wears his ring but cannot possibly love him as I do. Myself, I still have my pick of virtually any other man, except the only man—Tony. Yes, Fatima, you were right, some man finally did shatter my heart, but as I am a seamstress of hearts I will mend it and plan to have a good time living as close to the edge as a pendulum. The greatest successes of the Chicago Fire is the fact that it eventually went out. Toe was the match that lit that Chicago fire and then faded into my next life.

Tony is my Chicago fire, and he too will one day be as successful as the true flames! He will go out.

Skillet Brown

I best remember tomjack by his untimely visits to my Baltimore apartment in the slums on Monument Street. Right from the start, it was Mama and us three girls. Buttons was the eldest during this early sixties era. She was seven years old, with a big hooked nose and frog teeth. Buttons was also really smart like a professor or something. She was also as strong as Paul Bunyan's Babe, the blue ox.

My sister D. C. was eleven months younger than Buttons, real mean, but she looked okay.

At the time, I was four years old, a raving beauty for my age, and spoiled like grapes in a bootleg wine jar. Mama was young and separated from her husband, Toots and we three females were on our own.

Although we loved Mama dearly, we also loved it when she would go out to night school.

Ms. Luckie and Mr. Geoff was a white-haired couple who lived downstairs in the other apartment in our building.

Mama used to give them pretzels and raisins every time that they watched us while she went to night school. We never had any real fun at Ms. Luckie and Mr. Geoff's place, but we did get to watch good television shows.

As I think back further and through the years, I can remember when Mama's brother Detrick's eldest son, tomjack, had relocated from North Carolina to Baltimore. Tomjack was so short and skinny that he looked like a little boy with a big mustache. We used to laugh at his funny-looking features a lot. Still, we enjoyed listening to him talk. He used to drink a strong, smelly liquid from a bottle every day, and then fall to the floor yelling, "My momma's name is Skillet Brown . . . Skillet Brown . . . Skillet Brown . . . Skillet Brown," *Qqqqzzzz* . . . , then off to sleep this little thirty-five-year-old man would drift, reeking of his foul liquid.

It did not take me very long to figure out that tomjack was an alcoholic just like his girlfriend, Ms. Ginnette who lived with him. Ms. Ginnette was so funny to me. She had one brown eye and one blue eye and smelled just like tomjack. She was certainly no looker that's for sure.

Anyway, Ms. Ginnette used to fuss because tomjack liked to stay over our house so much. Every day, he would scratch the mustache that seemed to be bigger than his whole body and walk into our front door with the key that Mama had given him so that he could check on the house when we went to visit my aunt Mitsey over in the Bronx, New York. I thought it was really funny how sometimes Ms. Ginnette would follow tomjack fussing, and he would turn around and take his tiny fist and punch her in any area of her face until he drew blood. Buttons would sometimes yell to Ms. Ginnette that she hated for no reason, "Aha, Aha, you got puuuunched!" After several punches, Ms. Ginnette would run from our home crying, and tomjack would come into our home with Mama fussing at him for beating up Ms. Ginnette as if he had done something wrong. Buttons used to like the special attention that tomjack always paid to her whenever Mama was not looking. He used to throw kisses at Buttons and D. C., but never at me. I hated how tomjack paid me no mind. Tomjack would even sneak and give my two sisters nickels to dance for him when no one was looking. When they danced for him, they had to wear dresses or skirts and pull them high above their waist. I did not understand this. Did he not know that this made their underwear show? Tomjack did not seem to mind looking at their underwear. In fact, with Mama and me in the other room, I used to peek at him sticking his grubby little hands in the front open zipper of his pants and pulling out a really stiff eleventh finger with a hat made onto the tip of it. He would always show this finger to them as they danced. I guess this was a reward for them dancing for him. D. C. said that one time, tomjack had told them that this eleventh finger was a giant snake made onto his body. He said that he used it to make females cry and call him Daddy. I had not known that he had so many daughters. Why would they want to call him Daddy? Anyway, when he showed them his hooded snake, he would get mad with the snake just like he would with Ms. Ginnette except he would not punch it. Instead, he would start choking it in his fist using a back and forth motion. It was like magic when tomjack did this. The hat on the snake would keep on disappearing inside of his fist then keep appearing again like the game: now you see me, now you don't, now you see me, now you don't, as he would yank it faster and faster. Buttons used to say that he was spanking his monkey. He must have spanked his monkey pretty hard because he made it sick. After a couple of minutes, I would actually see the hood on tomjack's snake vomit up thick white vomit everywhere. Tomjack seemed to like it too. He would breathe real hard and then tremble like it was cold in the house while he was smiling with his head thrown back. For some reason, my sisters would never tell or let me tell Mama about the cute games that her first cousin tomjack played with Buttons and D. C. This made me start hating tomjack since he would not play those games with me too. Tomjack also played jokes as well as games. I knew this by the joke that he played on my two sisters one night when it was raining.

As clear as an after-the-rain sunshine, I can remember back to a cold, wet night during the Christmas school break. Tomjack had beaten Ms. Ginette so bad that night that the ambulance had to take her from their home. He then came over our house before the police could catch him. Mama was not at home, she was in night school, and we were downstairs with Ms. Luckie and Mr. Geoff. I can remember the rain coming down with the fury of a greased roller coaster that night. The thunder and lightning whipped the concrete city with the rage of a hungry cougar. It was on a Tuesday night, and Ms. Luckie and Mr. Geoff had sat down with us in front of their television to watch a comedy show when there came a rugged knock at the door.

"Who's dat," said Mr. Geoff, rising his old tired body up from the dirty red rocking chair in front of his living room television set. Ms. Luckie just sat beside us, eating raisins with us and laughing at the TV show that we were watching.

"It's me, Skillet Brown's son, Willie Brown," said tomjack's voice, coming through the door. I noticed that, for some unknown reason, tomjack was using his real name this time. As Mr. Geoff opened the front door, I heard tomjack tell him that my mother was back home and wanted him to bring us upstairs to our apartment.

The naive Mr. Geoff gathered the crumpled dinner bags that Mama had brought down to us and sent us with tomjack. For some reason that night, tomjack seemed to be in a hurry and rushed us up to our apartment. When we got there, he told us that he was a great warrior, and said "Watch this."

With that said, he took his small foot and kicked open our dirty mahogany door like the god of the rivers that I had already perceived him to be by his own will.

Even though we laughed at his tiny Peter Pan-toe shoe smashing the cross of the door, I did wonder why he needed to kick open the door if Mama was inside. In addition to this, he had his own key. *Ooooh*, Mama was gonna be so mad and would come a-running any minute now. She never thought that things were as funny as we did. Just as I was thinking these thoughts, tomjack suddenly stopped laughing and glared at me like I had robbed his stagecoach or something.

"Buttons and D. C.," he said, while still looking at me so mean, "go in the house, I will be right wiff you."

Obediently, they complied. As I stood puzzled, looking at tomjack, I could not understand why he did not want me to go into the house too. I could not help but wonder why Mama did not show up at the door. Was she really in the house?

Just as I was about to open my mouth and ask tomjack why I could not go in too, the answer to my lingering question migrated through the smelly troposphere like the creep in the footsteps of Adam's serpent in the Garden of Eden. Tomjack's eyes glared harder at me, colder than Titanic's iceberg. There was a distant, evil, and twisted look on his ugly, boyish face like I had only seen on him just before he would beat up Ms. Ginette. It was at this point that he spoke to me harshly and firmly.

"Beech, he said to me, you gotta big mouth, and I don't like you. Rose ain't home, I told a lie. She is around the corner waiting for you. Now you march your big-mouth self outta here and go look for her, for I beat you worst." At this point, I burst out crying.

Right then, a fist the size of a cannon ball shot out of the air like the sharp apparition of a filthy poltergeist and landed on my tiny nose and mouth. Out of nowhere, I saw beautiful colors and the American flag that we used in nursery school before I felt that excruciating pain that caused blood to shoot out from my nose and mouth like a meteor.

Tomjack must have forgotten and thought that I was Ms. Ginette.

I was so afraid as I snatched up the musty shirt that tomjack ripped from his foul body and tossed at me.

"Clean up the blood, and go find Mama!" he snapped angrily at me.

At this point, I didn't even know tomjack anymore. He was like a raged madman trapped in a blowing fire.

I fled as if tomjack was shooting at me or something.

As I was darting from the apartment steps, I saw tomjack quickly leap inside my door as if he had to use the bathroom. He did not even bother to close the door behind him.

I did not believe tomjack when he said that Mama was around the corner at night, and in the rain, thunder, and lightning. Besides, she never left us alone or sent us out alone at night. For this reason, I tiptoed back up the stairs to our three-room apartment. Still in furious pain and wiping blood from my swelling lips and my nose with tomjack's stinking shirt, I walked in to my home, straight through the kitchen, past the bathroom, and through the bedroom of my two sisters. I sneaked into the very last bedroom that I shared with my mother.

By now, tomjack had started my sisters dancing for him while he played the harmonica.

They were lifting up their dresses high above their heads and showing their underwear while they were dancing. They also had their back turned to him while they were dancing. Because tomjack's back was turned to me, he did not see me come in, neither did Buttons and D. C.

Secretly, I eased up under the double bed that Mama and I shared. I could see the entire room from there, and it was from there that I watched tomjack do strange things to my two elder sisters.

After playing for a little bit longer while my sisters danced, tomjack stopped suddenly and asked them a question.

"You know why I have all of the power like the god of the river?" he asked as he pointed to the hooded snake that he kept beneath the shiny brass zipper in the front of his pants.

He then answered himself and said, "'Cause my momma's name was Skillet Brown."

"Stop dancing you two bitches," he yelled to my two sisters.

I could not understand why tomjack always referred to us three girls as bitches. We had never been to the beach before, plus it was too cold outside to go.

After his remark, tomjack ran as if he had been struck by lightning to the front door and slammed it with the force of a category four storm.

"Where is Lynne?" yelled Buttons behind him, now sobbing for me.

"Oh, she decided to go back to Ms. Luckie's," lied tomjack as he reentered the room.

On this remark, an unreal haze of deception smoldered the entirety of the room like the soured sun after the so-called death of Jesus on the Cross, and our Lord took over the survival of Buttons and D. C.

At this point and what seemed like television slow motion, I peered at tomjack walking over to Buttons, squatting and looking up at her huge hooked nose. "You sure is ugly," he whispered naughtily to her with her unhurtable feelings. Before one could utter "Jack Rabbit," I witnessed tomjack as he suddenly stabbed a grubby, calloused hand beneath Button's dress and ripped off her underwear with one strong hand as if his first name was Jack, yeah like that guy called Jack the Ripper, or something. I was in shock and totally flabbergasted. I could not believe what my eyes were showing me. Still bleeding from the nose, but not mouth, I watched tomjack brutally twist an oily and stained handkerchief around the small mouth of my elder sister as she frantically fought for air and attempted to scream.

"If you bitches tell anyone what I am about to do to the two of you, Ima kill dat Momma of yours," laughed tomjack evilly. I was still in awe as I waited for the blazing pitchfork of this new monster to stab my two sisters' tiny hearts, but it never came. Instead, tomjack did them worst. It was not a pitchfork that he stabbed them with, but worst. While D. C. sat crouched in the corner in obvious and quiet fear as her turn for torture and humiliation was inevitable, tomjack suddenly took his grimy right hook and slammed it into one of the eyes of my shrieking helpless sisters. He beat my defenseless Buttons ferociously like she may have killed Skillet Brown or something. I laid flat on my stomach and bit my bottom lip until it bled again. I knew that no matter what I saw, I could not move or let it be known for any reason that I was in the room. If I did, I knew that I too would become a victim of whatever tomjack was going to do to my sisters. After all, he hated me. Within the seconds that represented hours, I saw tomjack use both hands to lift my trembling sister high above the foldaway cot on the other side of the room. Even though he was a little man, she looked so tiny, fragile, and scared in his hands. This time, tomjack's hands looked huge as Mount Everest as he lifted and dropped little Buttons on the cot. Before the cock could crow thrice, he was all over her body with his own now-naked body thrusting and grunting on top of her while he painfully twisted her tiny arms behind her back. She seemed to be in unbearable pain, trying to free herself from this ravishing, wild, torturing monster, and it was just no use. All the time that tomjack was hurting Buttons like this, he kept yelling, "My momma name Skillet Brown . . . Skillet Brown . . . Skillet Brown." He yelled over and over again until he suddenly arched his hairy back and leaped off of my bucking and heaving sister. He then reached out with a dirty ashy hand, grabbed Buttons by the hair, and flung her naked body to the cold hardwood floor as if she were a lifeless rag doll or something. One of her eyes was swelled up and bloody as big as tomjack's fist. Her entire facial features had changed from the beating that tomjack had given her . . . What had Buttons done to tomjack to make him so mad with her, and where was our Momma who was always so overprotective of us? Buttons was still heaving and began to vomit for what appeared to be hours. My tiny heart sank as

I watched tomjack run toward the erratic D. C., shriveled and shaking in fear in the corner. He was still yelling something about Skillet Brown as he grabbed D. C. by the hair, dragged her out of the corner, and whipped out a plastic container of baby powder by magic and began pouring it all over my child sister, turning her white like a ghoul as she screamed in terror. "Mama name Skillet Brown," he yelled again.

By the same magic and invisible pocket, tomjack whipped out a polluted bottle of liquid and took a fat gulp, he then poured it all over D. C. "Gotta clean you up like a little baby," said tomjack as he poured the poison on my D. C., "you done made a smelly."

It was then that I noticed the runny brown liquid running down my sister's legs. At that precise moment, I noticed that that snake with the hood on tomjack's belly was protruding, bloody, and stiff as a corpse as he cleaned it on D. C.'s cheek. Never ever had I seen my two sisters so helpless and so unprotected. Just before tomjack flung D. C. on the same cot that he hurt Buttons on, I watched tomjack swiftly kick Buttons in the stomach like she was a piece of trash while she lay bloody, heaving, and throwing up on the floor to get her out of the way so that he could get D. C. over to the small bed.

After getting her there, he savagely ripped off her dress and underwear and leaped on top of her.

"Please! Please!" I heard D. C. scream out in pain. "Whatever I did, I am so sorry. Please don't hurt me anymore." Tomjack ignored her and kept grinding and moving around while he tortured my six-year-old sister.

By this time, I could take no more. I squeezed my young eyes tight as the wings of the sparrows that glided across the midnight heavens that Mama had read about while I listened sometimes. There was a holy presence filling the contours of this room now, and I meant to use it. Remembering the prayers that poured from the pulpit like distinguished British tea in my heart and mind, I began to take control of the situation, and I prayed the only prayer that I knew, "Our father who art in Heaven Hallowed be thy name . . ."

By the time that I reached my amens, something that I will never forget happened.

That's right. Someone heard my mind talking to God. IT WAS MAGNIFICENT! No, It was called a MIRACLE!

There was a jerky crack in the screams of D. C., and our little shabby door burst open again with fever and rage. The first thing that popped inside was a gigantic cowboy gun that looked black like the ones that we would see on television. Behind the cowboy gun came fat whitish knuckles glued to a thick red hand. This was followed by a thick red-faced policeman with a pins and needles—looking hairdo. The longer I watched, the more I saw. Policemen were shooting through the door with pop guns and fat pogo sticks that seemed to move by themselves. I had never seen so many police officers before. The stick-haired police officer was the first to run over to tomjack, who had suddenly released D. C. and made an attempt to run.

Instead, Officer Stick-pin-hair darted through the atmosphere and wrapped a forceful rain-soaked bear hug around tomjack's small neck, and then came the "bitch" word again.

"Oh no, you summer bitch," he yelled through the commotion of the police billy clubs that had started beating tomjack unmercifully. "My babies," I heard Mama's voice cut in as I saw her heavenly and distorted face as she darted through the door screaming like I never heard her or anyone else scream before.

"Lynne, my baby," Mama screamed just as I got the courage to slide from under the bed.

"He didn't touch her," screamed the not-reincarnated Buttons as a man and woman in white suits helped Buttons and D. C. to their feet.

"Get them two babies to a hospital quick," yelled a stiff-necked officer who was still helping to beat tomjack's bloody, almost lifeless body as it lay curled up in a heap on the floor.

"Somebody help me," sobbed tomjack.

"Noooooooo!" he yelled, "My mama named Skillet Brown!" He yelled again as if he was trying to prove this to himself.

This was the last full sentence that I heard from tomjack as Mama released me quietly from her grip, and a shabby, dirty razor knife floated in slow motion from her hand to the already bloody neck and shoulders of tomjack on the floor. He then let out a ferocious scream, and a police officer snatched the knife from Mama's hand and gave it to my aunt Poochie Pie who was kicking tomjack's body on the floor.

"Did you see that? She cut his throat," yelled an excited and laughing police voice.

"Naw, she didn't," yelled another, "he fell on her straight razor!"

This was some night. The entire scene became hazy and misty until it faded into a few days into the future, and I found myself raising my head up from my mother's lap when she yelled to the doctor, "Syphilis! Syphilis! What do you mean he gave my babies syphilis?"

There were sobs and tears everywhere, but finally a smile when I heard Mama tell someone that tomjack got fifty-two years in jail flat time for raping my sisters and assaulting me. As the years passed, D. C. seemed to healthily go on with her life, but Buttons stayed withdrawn and fearful. The only time that she would smile full force was when Aunt Poochie Pie would tell us how tomjack got beaten unmercifully every day in the jailhouse for child sexual abuse. While tomjack was in jail, it was also discovered that he too had been a victim of molestation as a child. The molester was his mother. Her name was Skillet Brown.

FROM: RAPE BY CANDLELIGHT

Just a Part of the Hills

From the frosted window of my pink-flavored jeep
painted strawberries and cream,
can hear the telephone ring from the charioted kitchens
of my invisible palaces.
From the mistletoed door frame of my barn
that holds the silver eggs everyday Christmas
I can hear you calling my name inside
swirled-flashing, make-pretend, strobe night-lights.
As for me, I slouch down further in my hot pink jeep and make a dream.
With passion and warmth, I just may love them
dreams because I put you in them.
I feel I have transported you from the fleshy real world
to my own make-believe world.
It is a world that is guided by dragon snakes and podium queens in slums
inside the sea.
It is a world that unlike matter, I can create it, and I can destroy it.
My God! How I would love for you to be a part of this world.
With the magic of broom rides and dancing socks,
I can wave a bony stick and . . . pooF.
I can have rest. I can have peace. I can have life.
I can so have bodily privacy.
Ain't no other world of this esquired nation
like this for a lady on a journey.
Yeah, unlike Mr. King, I am en route.
I have not been a part of the hill in my search.
Yeah, was it in my search for God's promise
to a man known as Noah . . . the rainbow?
Do I not too deserve to live this young life
to the ultimate pleasure of man's full moon?
So slouching even deeper beneath my steering wheel,
I cancel you without restrictions.
No more quiet kisses in the night . . .

No more holding hands by black oil light.
No more vows of affection concealed,
no more sweet and righteous lies to my first loves.
My cinnamon-toed slippers press cotton-candied brakes,
and *VROOM*! I'm off to life.

To Love Me by the Light of Day
Love speaks so highly of itself like love from God's warm graces
not ever like the smothered kisses on youthful children's faces.
A Webster-type of love in love is as overt as the air
withholding not a secret love that all the world can share.
I know the man that I called Dad as loved as love could love
and never would he dare to hide this love from GOD above.
Love's not really love, one knows, while private, closed, or hidden
nor is love a real true love when all the world's forbidden
to see the special times we share or feel our passion too
and know our love from inside out like we as lovers do.
Go tell it on the mountaintops and far within GOD's sight.
There is no stronger lie of love than love confined to night.
Please love me just as well my love when skies are scraped with white
and pavement walkers stride by fields unburned by city light
that straddles cars or barn-side cows in daytime's open faces.
But never live the lie of love in secret hidden places.

Frosted Veils

He knew the woman's frosted hand
so longed for boyish heat
He knew that she would come again
to make her life complete
He knew her by her Porsche's bright lights
up on his bedroom wall
and she would come invade his nights
and steal his flesh and all.
The eerie sounds of icy palms
would trail his stairway rail
Then all at once the sitter's arms
were blankets for the veil.
The veil that closed up little boy's eyes
on nights that he should see
and froze the tongue that calls the wise
who dare to set him free
from demon kisses by the yards
too grown-up for his soul,
and not in sync with baseball cards
and cowboy hats of gold.
What if he knew a parent-friend
could lift the frosty veil
That hid beneath the coat of sin
That waltzed along his rail?

ORDER THE WORLD

The order of this world of mine is candied china plates
and Mama's new exotic stole and staying up too late,
My stickers from Ms. Beesler's class
and paste up on the looking glass.
The order of this world will say my crayon's never blunt
and I eat laughing soup that laughs whenever I have lunch.
And my friend Tarla has a cat. She chose to name him "Nice"
'cause he sits upon the outside pond and wait for Christmas mice.
It's me who's free to smell the smell of fresh-cut city pines
and hang my suit for pool time fun on Mama's clothing lines.
It's me who's free to love the child who lives inside of me,
the little girl that lives in here is for the world to see.
I love to love or live to love the order of this world
No interruptions in this youth need ever be unfurled.
Someone, I know, has paid the price to keep my childhood pure.
Who said the love of twisted men should kneel here at my door?
A child should always be a child as long as youth allows
and stay immune to all that breaks the sacred childhood vows
No man of men should touch this youth or taint my childhood joy
The freedom to be young belongs to every girl and boy.

Unfought Revolutions

Something inside me burned in my chest
when he spoke words that were not so holy.
His foreign mouth made unfamiliar sounds
that coincided not with my world.
By the grace and the God of a God who is God,
I shied from the temples of my body.
I feared his words would soon prosper
and become physical upon my innocent flesh
for which he lusted without reservation
or justification of my little girl nature.
Lord of my Lord—my world was a soothing cascade
of perfumed water to fill tea cups.
My world was about Suzy's paper summer cut-out skirts
and Mama's ice cream cologne.
At what point did the lust of adult boy fulfill
the needs of a child in her critical years?
Did he not know the historical burden
that would trail my life for the rest of my life?
Did he not care that my epitaph would reflect
the sadness of a compromised world;
a world in which I carried the guilty face
of the abused abuse of the abuser?
I guess no . . . and that night I awaited for
Lucifer's sharp mouth upon my hushed tongue
and to be held in unholdable places
and I dared not suffer myself to feel.
I longed for someone to know that he came to me
in tangible dreams by day by night.

And I longed to discover just what fitted his
prevaricating love into my cherubic world.
Now that the season for his lust is no more,
my old heart is no less a victim of his own.
My pain is my flower watered by my own tears
and thus it grows and grows and it grows.
My old painted head will forever rest with the pain
of a soldierless revolution that was never fought,
but still perishing in battle in my calming heart.

Electric Rain

He said to me, "You'll never tell or snakes will watch you roam
You dare not be a foolish fool when Mom and Dad are home."
Speak too low with layman's tongues and while secrets tend to shy
away within the jaws of kids who learn to live this lie.
So well within the deep of night, I vowed to never speak
of all the love Dave had for me by night of every week.
He said no man's this girl should tell for I was guilty too
and I should learn to live this lie as Christians often do.
As blameless as the serpent's tongue in Eden's sacred gate,
I swore an oath I'd keep for life regardless of my fate.
The metamorphic days of weeks somehow became the months
and I beheld the whitewashed lie so much more than once.
Then once when snowman season left, I cuddled by the phone
and heard my mommy tell a friend she'd brought a present home.
The present was for me she said to have for all of times
I never had to share this toy. She said it was all mine.
I learned that it would say to me whatever I would say
It never had a freelanced word that I could find to play.
It sizzled like the rain outside, repeating after me.
Electric sounds of my own voice was all it seemed to be.
I learned that I could tell it all since it was only me.
It was not man's or other man's as far as I could see.
Now keeping David's vows each day, I spoke of love we had
and placed this special part of me beneath my sleeping bed.
I told me of the pain I felt whenever he was near
and how I longed for help to come and take away my fear.
Like magic from my fairy books and Christian vows of faith
my shattered heart appeased with dreams somehow was now in place.
For deep within the beams of dawn, I watched my mother weep
and while she held my private rain that helped me get to sleep.
Then precious men in blue that day had asked me of Dave's lie
and kept me safe from all the pain that always made me cry.

Then Mama held me tight much more and chased away the hurt
The name of Dave became a ghost and perished with the dirt.
I never knew just how the men could know how I had sinned.
As I had vowed, I told no one but my electric friend.
Within the depths of aging pain which has a different name,
I watch my Willie play inside with his electric rain.
No mans of men could touch his flesh for sizzling codes of red.
All kids should have electric rain beneath their sleeping beds.

Solace of the Ocean

I rinsed my flesh with scotch and creme in moon-hot winter air
The stench of love all over me was more than I could bear
I stooped upon the windy beach and swiped a fist of sand
I smelled the dew of mist and lust in grains inside my hand.
In grains and weed that washed my soul that night beside this sea
behind my Asian raisin bun and jar of herbal tea.
I sat and ate and sipped that night and scrubbed my body clean
with faded fist of moon-bleached snow inside the water's beam.
Within the fuzzy smoke of dawn, I watched the hawk birds' cry
I loved to see the ripples dance whenever they flew by.
I counted fingers, toes, and feet and algae from the sea.
I passed the time away for joy of all that's dear to me.
Last night, a poisoned touch of love defiled this sacred temple.
Tonight, I wash and cleanse a lie I choose not to remember.
I felt I'd never feel the strength in womanhood he stole
or taste the pleasure of a "No" from lips still in control.
And now I lift my polished lamp to view the gliding waves.
I twitch an itching nose to smell the perfumed water blades.
A woman's pride is all she has when all has been forsaken.
The beauty of the waterside blocks out the pain I've taken.
Residues of my bath and dine I place now on the beach
and lie beneath a jeweled sky and wait for God to speak.
In solitude, I lie awake to hear my only friend
guide me through this Judased life as healing thus begins.

Do You Ever Feel the Need to Fall in Love with Love?
Always leaving your date with a gentle hug.
Taking into account the fate of "No" in her voice.
Every day knowing that this lady claims choice.

Remember you know the temple of our Savior.
Always knowing how to curve your behavior.
Please also find the title of this rhyme.
Entered in the first letter of every line.

PRIVATE ZONES

At home today, I took a branch and made a Mr. Tree
You should have seen his woody face, he looked a lot like me.
Like me when something's wrong with wrong
when something's out of reason
Like me when trouble comes to call and something's out of season.
I stuck a fancy beeper friend upon his private wall.
His breast, his hips and thighs, and tuck beneath his belly ball.
I placed a fancy beeping bulb upon his lower back.
I put a funny flashing light beneath a forward sack.
Now everywhere I placed my lights, no human being could touch
For it they did, my glowing friends would buzz and beep so much
that all the world would come to know my private zone's been heard,
and I myself will learn to tell and never say a word.
We all should have a Mr. Tree to show our special parts.
We all should learn the path on us for which the beeping starts.
With Mr. Tree, we come to learn from head down to our toes
which parts of us is just for fun and what's our private zones.

The Lull After the Storm

Casually I'm bending at the top of your bed.
I'm told that you bow to a king.
I'm stroking the crown at the base of your head
and loving the pleasure this brings.
Through lamps like Aladdin's, I'm watching you sleep
as cloudy warm slumber will breathe.
Yet eyes drawn too tight says you're counting your sheep
and your rest is not guided by peace.
Oh, man in my life, I love you too much
and I know that you suffered in vain
My guy, you must learn that the people you trust
are sometimes the source of your pain.
But time is a healer, you live for hereafter
and now, man, your life must go on.
The rain of your tears is replaced by your laughter
and the lull is now after the storm.
At peace with your nature, forgetting past time,
your highness, come back to your throne.
Mature like the tart in the age of old wine,
my king, you must learn to be strong.
A body once ravished, the core of raw sin,
is a time that no time can erase
My man, you must learn how to reign once again
and learn to keep your face with your faith. We know that the flesh of a
man has depowered his heart and his soul never changed.
The man must march on for all that will follow
and always remember his name.
I'm casually bending at the top of your bed
It's time that the world kissed your ring.
Caressing the crown on the crown of your head,
I'm watching a new king called king.

SOLDIERS, AS YOU WERE

There is a pacified quietness in the chilled and immaculate evening air.
It is holy like a sense of peacelike peace that waits
for GOD and no other man.
Through the smoking spy clouds that live
between the emancipated trees in deep forest,
I see the shadows of disillusioned youths that hide
from themselves in foxholes at dark.
They hide like invalid molehills behind outspoken
sticks of hot Georgia rain in spring.
They hide like winter groundhogs that roam at
night on the haunted banks of watersides.
They hide like the molested soldiers of shame that
they have somehow come to be.
They hide with the reservations of tainted warriors in a world
they once ruled without sin.
And I'll be damned if I choose not to deliver
a helping hand in pity and speak,
"Soldiers as you were in these filthy dungeons of
Gomorrah that we call our world."
"Soldiers as you were, armed with the dirty weapons
of freedom in a world obsolete.
The time for defeat is no more. Live, soldier, as
I once have lived and I now live again."
You are Uno and Eine in the revolution of life,
you are the first, and you are the first,
the noble in honor, certainly no less than man
or woman knights in glimmering coats, coats of armor
that rest on strong shoulders of fearless
warriors that prey on simplicity.
Captains! as you were on your feet!
and above my command, marching as down Zion.
You are wise like elusive cardinals that hop
from raindrop to spraying raindrop at dusk.
You are wise beyond your years, your youthful
temples stained gray with knowledge.

You are a veteran of pain that unselfishly
breeds pain, pain, and eventually, wisdom.
There is a wordless song in your heart right now,
one without melody, sound, or tune.
Tonight, you will sing it to the whistles of you own piper.
You will redo your life by it.
Ain't no shame in shame, so dance to it as you will,
and be at peace with peace again.
Through all principalities and the imposition of time,
soldiers! you are the mountaintop.
Esquire of my sentimental world, my precious soldiers,
I want you as you were, and as you will be.
Soldiers! I want you as you have been unleashed from all tribulations.
Soldiers, I want you as you were!

THE LIKES OF ME

You asked me freely in a month called May
when I would cease to worship the vanity in my love for the likes of me.
Within this time, I thought to you I would say,
"Never, Mr. Captain sir, have I not dropped
these bleached love anchors out to my sea
and rode the high waves to the beach of this heart?"
Now I belong to me. I can and I do now love
the cracking of spring winds against my blue hairpins
as I sit fraternizing with male friends in my summer kitchen in June.
Being me, Free to love me with a selfish and
unprofitable love at the footstools of Satan.
Yes me, with my diverse boiled rose stems in
red bags of white tea on church days.
Yes, me, with my emancipated first laugh of freedom
when the kids are grown and gone.
I can choose to find humor in the elements of fog lights in European
Audies in snow and I can now have my baked chicken wings
with white cheese and Spanish apple pie.
Because I have learned to love the likes of me,
I can do as I please, whenever I please.
No more binding ties to hold this little girl captive. I have accepted and
taken me for what and whom I have chosen to be after the hail in this
life. I am elusive and reserved for me, under me, with me, and only me.
Yeah, me, with my scorching fancy to be bold in tongue and in touch
with myself. Me, right here on copper pedestals and the threshold of the
GOD of a GOD who is the only GOD,
and with a complex like that GOD.
It is the likes of me who have cupped the sweat of the
holy and wise in antiquated hands.
It is the likes of me who have learned to live in a life
unmade by man or calamity.

My vanity is my own for the keeping for as long as
I may taste the salami of this world.
It is as disrobed as the fire and the passion in my verse
and in my song and in my heart.
Never! Under a talcum powered sun or the
tear-polished moon of woman will I cease to
abolish the vain love of freedom and self-worth relished
within the likes of this soul,
. . . not even for the likes of me.

THE HEALING OF THE ROSE BUSH

I have never really minded cool winter snow in a
June or December growling rain.
Different and versatile as this here lady may be,
I have even been partial to pain
I used to sneak down to foaming rivers to snack
on my wine cakes and bread
remembering the day that you left me and
the fountains of tears that I shed.
I shied from the world like a ski slope, I sobbed and I waited to die.
Psychotic, and twisted and hurt to hot fervor,
I watched as slow time would pass by.
I gripped at the wild-blowing burning that seem
to blaze cold in my chest
I knew that my loss was forever and I would just settle for less.
But still then one day with GOD's mercy, I felt the faint smell of a rose
as I cried on wet earth I now fancied, fresh flowers surrounding my nose.
I never knew life to be sweeter as I noticed the dirt on my toes.
I kind of felt foreign and weary just rubbing the mud from my clothes.
Just why was I starting to feel more when I should be reeking in pain.
Who let in a mere crack of sunshine when
life was just drenching with rain.
A message of light seemed much broader as
I learned how to resee the world.
Each day was a new day of challenge like searching
for the dams with the pearl.
I feel I began to feel feelings and the smell of new life all around.
From the sassy gold skies beneath heaven
to the sweetest white clay on the ground.
I learned to taste apples and popcorn on cool nights
at home in my room.
I learned as I danced to dance music in mystical sounds of the boom.

The world was becoming my lobster. My life was no longer its shell
As I learned the old beeps of a pager and to answer my ringing doorbell.
And now I go down to the waters to gulp down
fresh wine cakes and bread
forgetting the day that you left me and mountains of tears that I shed.
I now know my life has a purpose and the smell of the rose is not in vain.
I've learned to live life in sweet essence and never remember your name.

PASADENA LIGHTS

I feel I did know you sometime in the past,
the kinglike air in the way that you laugh,
the nobleman arch in the small of your back,
firm fingers around a Parliament pack.
The earl of strong shoulders that rested at nights
on poles we once called our Pasadena lights,
with all of the flavor of regal monsieurs
you beamed through the crowd like drunk tides at shores.
And after work hours in the cool Maryland breeze
I watched you men gather beneath streetlights and trees.
I loved you in silence from life's depths to its heights
and the warm way you shone beneath those streetlights.
Elusive like sin in the dark of my room
under Pasadena lights and a whitewashed moon
lance loved a king without heartache or shame
I so loved a man who knew never my name.
A year and then many I still room alone
behind a dimmed window and ringless cell phone.
Behind a hushed tongue with too much to say
while watching my life and my love waste away.
I needed to tell you I loved you those nights
that I watched you in awe beneath the streetlights.
I fear that my love has altered my sanity
thanks to the shy death of a heart led by vanity.
Last night when I woke from a sweet lustful dream,
I fled to the window to look for my king.
I tripped on the buckle of a free-laying sandal
I searched through haze of my freshly lit candle.
By the glow of the dawn, I thought I did see
the figure of royalty outreaching to me
through the powdered rainfall and cool Maryland nights
I look for you still beneath the streetlights.

With time as my Judas, I lie down to rest
with heaviest burden on top of my breast
now cursing the passing of unuseful time
when I should have chosen to speak my own mind.
I knew that I loved you sometime in the past,
the kinglike air in the way you laughed
the way that you glanced at my window each night
while waiting beneath our Pasadena lights.

Loving You between the Roars

Like each and every day by God, I waited at my gate,
bag of garbage in my hand—no fate.
Like every single day by God I'd see your shining face
pass me by with blowing kiss.
Warm kisses that made passionate love to the
candied winds ever so seductively at dawn.
Hot kisses that came in time for sweet rains in May,
carnivals in fall, soft snow then sun.
I'd wait in awe for the first roar of the garbage truck
when your loving face would appear.
Leading the trashmen my blessed way like
the pied piper of a grand new day.
By second roar, you would have passed all
by my watery knees and throbbing heart.
I would toss my bag in can and run back to bed
for the love of a heavenly man.
Now this withering hand and sanctified pen
can only write of our cherished tale of love.
The seasons here for you are no more by
Grace of a far and teasing Denver school.
Still, no less in love, I rise each day with garbage bag
in aging fist—in search of your smile.
Through festivals in summer rains and
December showers—twisted, confused, and lonely.
Do you ever feel how your Juliet cries out in pain
by the second roar of the garbage truck?
I feel the telepathy of a quiet passion from smoking
Colorado Plains to Dixieland Blue.
This lady's missing you from toilet-watered oils
in your hair to white-socked holy toes.
This rushing butterfall in my chest, where pieces of my heart
once lived says come home.
Now I listen for the third roar of the garbage truck—crushed bag
in tainted tear-stained fist.

I'll not have you crying on the other side of the mountaintops
with vain partiality for me.
I feel a bruising fancy to hold you as snugly
as you do me inside of principles or miles
especially in exotic and fine-cologned nights
which now it seems I smell. Lord, is it you?

THE MARYLAND GENTLEMAN

I sometimes recall an unselfish love to be loved by all men
somewhere within the autobiography of my slain youth.
Oh, what a prize I have been to the Maryland gentleman
or the alternative lifestyles of the other girl's lust for me
—a tantalizing ten in the warm bosom of this fragranced flesh . . .
and a GOD-carved Venus of dazzling beauty and Northern grace.
Oh, what a charm I have been to the Maryland gentleman
in the climax of impeded lives in an altered world.
Me, with my Rapunzeled locks of fine black hair
oiled with French kisses from passionate young men.
Me, with my casual brown eyes and seductive curved hips
that once loved free love in the temples of a city called Sodom.
Me, with my aromatic strong and womanly thighs
glistering and polished by the tears of many green ladies-obsolete,
and me with the temptation of a serpent in Eden's castle
has been no cross to the strong and proud Maryland gentleman.
Yes, me, with my seasoned thin curls of lukewarm hair
that reeks of the tears that I shed on the thighs of many young ladies.
With the fading slow life of casket-hound beauty
that slumps over the boundaries of a tattered cane.
Oh, what a prize I long to be for the Maryland gentleman
in these last two grains of sand left in my hourglass.
In this tired heart, there will never be an epitaph on this lovelife.
Maybe just a quest to be held by my love—
the gentle Maryland gentleman.
Now somewhat I feel that I still recall,
a selfish love to be loved by all men.
Oh, what a prize I have been to the Maryland gentleman
and the object of the forked tongue that said, she aged and need no love.
Still, traitorous time could not smother an even stronger lust for the
Maryland gentleman.

Not Meant to Dream Castles

I'm not meant to dream castles
with my white lacy negligee accentuating female curves
in my ballroom each night.
I had not meant to be bold when I asked your name
by reservoir-side

and this dazzling lady tipped from the throne room
with the eighth deadly sin in her cup.
I had not meant to feel sheltered when you took me in your man-arms
stroking your warm hair with the clean neck of a
woman's love in a perfected world.
I had not meant to be strong.
I had not meant to dream castles
when I wore your gold ring and I bore your boy babies
with the crying of Eve out in sin.
I had not meant to be the hunted of hunters and
never the hunter of games.
It was I who meant not to cook sweet sauces from Paris
and wash your fine hosen with the sweat of my foremama's in love
with the love of the love of injustice that kneels in the cockpit of pain.
I had not meant to taste rain.
I had not meant to dream castles
while constantly bickering with romance devoured by flames
that cremates the passion that once was the
virtue of luve, not pain, not pain.
Nor had I meant to sniff white tulips in cold summer weather
or see myself safe to the door
in formaldehyde smells of tainted romances
that made peace with the winds and left
not meaning to dream castles anymore . . . no more.

TENNESSEE SKIES

If I were the picture of deepness,
I'd sit on the threshold of heaven and sigh.
Diamond-shaped eyes of aging beauty that gazes at cosmic Tennessee.
The sun will waltz up from the waters
at the metamorphous of a fresh new day
merely to silhouette the last residues of an antiquated moon that's fading
and gliding away into a feigned tomorrow and the dusk of today.

If I were a picture of wonder, I'd kneel by the ocean and sing.
I'd smile with the rapport of Southern rapture
beneath the concepts of morning clouds.
Goblet in fist . . . to capture the fourth drop
of morning dew from rainbow in August.
So it's been said that the first three washes white,
the earth, but all others belong to me,
by grace of infinity, there's no such thing as tomorrows,
just reincarnated yesterdays.

The Tennessee sky is too regal—
like Sistine ceilings of Diego under GOD's moon
over quadrilateral beams of conceiving red clouds
obsessed with perfumed dews.
Dews that drip with the faint sound
of the cracked seahorns in a confederate South
only to burst softly upon leaf by glistening leaf
in this holy-warm and sentimental earth.
It is then that a breathtaking orange temple called sun rises to the
occasion of a new day.

It is then, with a complex like Oedipus,
that I long to control my Tennessee skies,
a God-created cosmic treasure where only my heart
has surely been—my flesh, left behind.
But if I were the picture of deepness, I'd rest at the dashboards of shores,
watching sunrise from misty rivers exploding with exotic burst of
repeated yesterdays.
But fresh and alive and unvanquished like only my Tennessee skies.

Inspired by Elder G. Warren Thompson
(Sanderson Memorial Church of the Living God
Radcliff, Kentucky)

MS. ADDIE'S HOUSE

Throughout this life I can recall Ms. Addie's comely bench.
We sat and ate Thanksgiving goose and smacked on buttered mint.
We sopped white gravy with our bread and carved our turkey deep
and slurped our pudding with our straws before the crust could leak.

Then after food, we'd hug and kneel as friends will often do.
And dare to sing Thanksgiving tunes until our tongues turned blue.
Ms. Addie's house just bloomed with love and peace from roof to floor.
We lived to feel a rush of love as we walked through her door.

No pleasures in this sainted world could ever find the way
to make our hearts just leap with fun as like Thanksgiving Day.
We sat, we ate, we socialized, we laughed so hard, we cried.
We never had an angry word no matter if we tried.

The season for Ms. Addie's house has somehow come and gone,
but all that's left of what we had within my heart lives on.
I gather what I meant to say was peace came once a year.
Inside the warmth of plastered walls where friends were cuddled near.

Now still within Thanksgiving Days, Ms. Addie's house lives here.
But still I lust Thanksgiving joy throughout each lifelong year.

Inspired by Rosa L. Nobles Vines and Addie Beatrice Calvert

If I Could Be so Bold

If I could be so bold tonight, I would lift my
"Heart of the Ocean" watching
your strong face,
knowing that a wise man stands just over my shoulder reaping what he never sowed.
And knowing that he is thus ordained by our natural father to lead his family home.
Knowing that he is casual king who is a blessed decision maker in the life of a woman.
He overrides all rituals or Freudian egos that has been the object of childhood values.
Values . . . that went not down in the sea when the boat did rock, and Jesus did sleep.
If I could be so bold tonight, I would lift an unprevaricating tongue and claim
the journey in the man as I follow him from the naked cracks below the troposphere.
Above the tingling and white-coat plains
of a prevailing heaven that is ours
for the taking,
clinging to the extravagant and masculine tail
of his shirt with dignity and
lifted chest,
forsaking the rain, trusting him blindly, trusting him beyond Mama's nurturing breast, trusting him with my sacred life, with a touch like Midas that has turned my heart to gold.
If I could be so bold tonight, I would squeeze his ironclad hands into mine
until they dripped with the freshness of the royal blood of virgins in flight to their knees.
Knowing that he is the esquire of this lady's heart beyond ALL others . . .
I am his Venus.

Though I wear my blazing candle in the pit of my chest at the inquisition of his name,
and though my girlish knees will buckle, melt,
and faint as smoking gelled
water
when I still smell his sweet breath inside the crab apple trees in March, I dare not flinch.
If I could be so bold tonight, I would chance to be forever free against his hard chest,
against his firm and buckled muscles during impulsive storms without breath or lull.
Like somewhat all men, the guy is drenched with the wisdom of the wisest
of all time,
and through informal promises to love him not, or little white sins that never mattered,
my submissiveness reigns with his highness—master under Christ in this spellbound world,
A borrowed world that belongs to all men who can love with passion the woman who
holds his brass pedestal through it all as he guides her by the glittering rays of GOD.

Remembering Maryland Knights

I watched you from the pews of home
and I never knew your name.
A soggy cough that came by phone
and I knew you just the same.

Remembering now the Maryland champ
in silhouettes of my mind,
I lift my fragranced yellow lamp
to see who's left behind.

No, I'll not bear this cross again
nor sob this journey long,
and I'll not dare to hear your pain
in soundless nights at home.

At twilight's dusk I'll peer to see
through misty panes of glass,
and know you as you really be
outside your capes of brass.

Remembering now the Maryland knights,
I passed you by in vain
inside the smoke of shipyard lights
and powdered Northern rain.

I never smelled your Newport swirls
nor touched your perfumed palms.
I'd know you by your plumstone pearls
and ball chains on your arms.

Remembering now the Maryland knights,
I'll paint my dickey blue
and work beside you day by night
and learn to know you too.

I rest my holy corporate pen
and burn my oil lamps bright
and chance to meet a brand new friend
I've known now all my life.

Shadows in My Wick

There is a shadow in my wick—my oil lamp shows
aplenty when a woman is lonely.
Still I lay resting on pastel coats from your
girlfriend's most precious linen,
listening to winter butterflies soaring above lullabied snowtaps
from my open window.
In rim sleep, I visualize the vision of the man
I've loved for seven painful years now.
But you're just a shadow in my wick.
Damned you, Adonis! I'm too tired to cry, though
I know she is locked in your arms now.
Those are your wet kisses at the bridge of her soft nose
on romantic nights at home . . .
Windy nights when I cry off to sleep alone longing
to hold you in these empty arms . . .
Just once forever, aware that there are seven tears
for each love year at the rainbow's end.
But they are shadows in my wick.
My fate with the man I so love is a sad pot of gold it seems,
but may I tell you my name?
Within the cheap chirps of crickets coming in from
the cold on an average icy night,
I listen wall to thin wall at your slow breathing in her
honorable and seductive ear.
Time's the fool of no man's who peers at the world
through Coke bottles in English fog.
Time is merely a shadow in my wick.
And thus I know that in time she will be your wife, and
I will be alone—me and my wick.
I know that I have shed many a tear as I watched her
dilated shadows ballet in your eyes.

Yes, eyes that love that special lady king of your heart
with the heat of volcanic fervor.
So deep into the neck of this unconsummated night,
I can still smell traces of you two
as I stand not the inkling of a chance? . . .
you are silhouettes in my wick.
The warm smell of bilirubin pumps to my heart as
I lift my cut-stoned cup and toast.
Here's to seven years alone that I went down in battle
defeated like a stickerless rose.
Here's to serenades in a blowless wind that whistles
sweet nothings in my soundless ears.
And to subliminal romance that blooms in fifth season
each year by light of my oil lamp
And here's to soft-drawn blanks, and casual nothings,
but shadows in my wick . . .

Concerts of Passion

Your voice is the voice of songs in my world.
It is brighter than heaven's moon jades in midnight air.
It is breathless like chimed mistletoes just before Christmas.
When the wind is at its lightest . . . when the wind is at its sweetest.
It is consuming and kingly in a nature that surpasses all of humanity.
It is teasing and tantalizing to the soul of a daughter
in love with your music.
The masculinity of your beautiful song is the bandit of this lady.
Though you turn your gifted head and sigh,
or drop by my place unknowingly,
I'll not turn away from the whirlpool of sadistic passion
for the verse of my own.
I'll not cease to dance to your tunes behind the huckleberry trees in
spring.
Were I merely the congenital scapegoat of your cherished voice,
I would be at peace.
And never under glimmering bodies of man's heavens
would I not feel rage in your song.
Dad, there is a raging concert in your beautiful heart.
I hear it in your songs.
It is soft but bodacious, like sleeping roe beneath our seas.
Like the crisp popping of faint autumn rain in June . . .
It's diverse, new, and alive
like the climax in the passion of old lovers
on warm sunny nights in winter.
It roars out to your audience with the fervor of majesty.
You sing my body to comfort.
You sing to me with the voice of the voice of real song in an infinite
world conceived by the vitality of your beautiful song.

ANGELS WITHOUT WINGS

Somewhere inside the pitch and the darkness,
by the light of day, to you a child is born.
He is tiny—she is twisted like intensified roe that slumbers
on the shores of haunted seas.
Seas that universal men sailed with desiderata in heart
to conquer compromised worlds.
Somewhere beneath the warm and sacred promise of the rainbow
by the immaculate rays of GOD's angels
My glimmer of jade called child soars as high
as low as melodious winds of peaks
Still loved by the mothering eyes of subliminal slits in infinity.
We call the world.
You were born without the wings of the commonest angel.
Why do you fly like the comrades we choose?
I watched in grace as you spread them,
peacocked wings that you have not
and glazed the frosted white skies with the
complex of cobblestone—none existing.
And I beheld wingless brown angels
They need no wings—they fly with their hearts
They fly side by side in an unreserved heaven
with the gentle winged swan-child.
They fly inside the antiquated evening and elusive mornings
in the fifth season of each year.
In unison with world harmony,
They need not wings for valor
They need not wings to devour the deep, mysterious,
and prevailing seas at shores.
They are child—no less than the diverse play of
children in castles of blue
So be not afraid of the frosted angel without wing or with wing.
My GOD has called the precious name of angels without wings.

Journeys of the Man

I watched you in silver silence as you marched
through the caving glaciers called street,
got your fine crown in your strong and leading hand,
guiding the kingdom of woman.
By the authority of my Lord and master,
I should follow you beyond this rounded earth.
The wand of holy matrimony has you bursting
with wisdom of a gardenless Adam.
There is and there will be no other but you below my God.
I must be subject to you.
Oh, leader in my life, I give allegiance to your borrowed rib,
as the source of my breath.
Yes, strong leader of chivalry, honor, and strength—arms
like flagpole raised as you march.
Outspoken chest of precious gem, I know you know
the way to the glory we seek.
Humbled by your manly voice and your God-fearing nature,
I now take your hand.
The fog in my life is thick, choking, and overwhelming,
but husbands know the way.
I will trust you blindly with heart in hand
to bring my life in from the husky cold.
Through the unwavering smog of sin and
ordained by our God, man, you shelter me.
Through this journey, I bypass a loving Mom,
an unblemished Dad, and all the world.
My painted lips whisper sweet thank yous to him
who loved me first, but I'm now taken.
Through this magical and blessed journey,
I'll not once lift my blindfold to see Your face.
I need only to feel the presence of my Lord
guiding my anointed keeper called husband.

My trust knows no measured boundaries, my man—show
me whom I'd not forsake for you.
Sheltered from the umbrellaless blowing rain of
innocent sin in raging fog, my man,
I follow you blindly through this deep, dark,
and chilling journey bearing no murmurs.
No weeping, no pain, no fear, without doubt,
uncertainty, or breach of trust, I know you,
and I know that beneath the booming and thunderous
brown heaven's man will lead me,
within this sweet journey, my man will bring me safely
to the comforts of a home called home.

Within These Walls

Within the scented halls of my church home church, I hear your tone.
Your elegant blessed tongue speaks the philosophy of the only God.
Then in the congregating silence of Christian virginity
I can smell your honor
as you sink to your holy knees to worship a jealous God
at an altar never built by man.
Within this goldlike cathedral over plastered white wall,
I somewhat taste your righteous tears, and you cry out to your savior,
leaving a philosophical sweetness at the base of your sacred tears,
forming the soft heat of a youthful sainted head that is aged in the knowledge of Christ.
Within heighty carved walls of a castle called Venus,
or church I see Godlike hands.
The warm and telepathic fingers of the
Nightingale drips with sugared waters.
Lord, Lord, sweet water with the aromatic name of
Christ by which you wash feet.
With which you spike the heavenly blood of
God with God by pleasure of God.
Within the jeweled belly of Jonah's whale, I too have time to think.
I feel the molecular conjugation of every atom of ecstasy as you preach,
I feel a voracious and insatiable hunger to know that
there is no death—only life in reverse.
My God-carved Rocket Jharoda called Pastor,
I follow your scepter within these walls.

WHITE LIKE BLACK SHEEP

I feel I do see you in a casual vision—rare like
Neptune in the limelights of heaven,
strong, laminated, and cherished by those who love GOD,
and just common man.
So misunderstood by understanding
and world peace . . . so mistaken by chaos.
If I see you beyond hot coconut trees in May
or ski lifts in white January, I see strength.
Am I too within the eyes of a nation who
has conquered not with passion, prejudice,
who has succumbed not to the tearing of the
foreign shirt under acid moons?
I feel I do see you in the image of the regalist of kings
who breathe by the lungs of GOD.
Intriguing, influential, and holy, with the suffering of
Christ in your blessed veins.
So full with the maturation of Christiankind
in a world that teases the strong.
While man's silver chariots blast aflame
with the motif cocktails of worldly sin,
I can hear you run from Potiphar's wife, no . . .
no temptation in your special garden.
You are lifted in body, spirit, and mind on your jaded
pedestal with all your gifts in lap.
My holy brother, you are dearly nobility on
the soothing soil upon which you stand
—firm right hand, bearing the inscription of wisdom
and self-worth in your sainted palm.
If ever our sun rises by light of fresh sweet oceans,
it does so in honor of your smile.
Never doubt yourself as the honorable king
that you have come to be in a world by you.
So if ever this lady who knows you by name will never
know your name with the world,
by way of God under grace of this baptized pen,
please know that the world loves you best.

Winters Like Home

Wintertime has come around in ole Kentucky blue.
The trees have shed their murdered leaves, the sky looks hazel too.
The cardinal birds still live outside within the winter chill.
The plants will have a hint of frost instead of overkill.
A mohair shirt, a satin scarf, an earmuff here and there
Is all I need to keep me warm in bluegrass winter air.
No sleds, no skates, no rubber boots, a flake or two of snow
Is all that keeps the winters cool and makes the season grow.
Oh, how I miss my winters home when skies are scorched with white.
Where singing birds have flown their coops and grass is not in sight.
Four feet of snow and blizzards too in winter caravan
With skis, with sleighs, with skates and hills just like in Pikes Peak land.
I really miss how hard we worked to build our snowmen strong.
With snowball fights beneath streetlights, we played all winter long.
There's just one joy at summertime we yearned throughout the year
The every day that tiptoed by as winter would grow near.
Now wintertime has come around in old Kentucky blue
With snowless hills and pseudo chills, there's not much here to do.
Wake up, I say, and smell warm frost in cool Kentucky air.
There's nothing great as winters home. No winters can compare.

AN AUNT NAMED MILDRED

(A dedication to my aunt, Mildred Lee Shamberger)

The candle flickers and spits at draping shadows on papered walls,
and I see the image of a singing phone that calls me within the night.
Could it be the lady knight in the life of this woman?
I say hi, and she comes to me with the sweetest voice
of an angel named Pluto.
It is my sacred aunt . . . my Mildred with a crown on her head,
with jewels at her feet.
My sizzling hot blood is boiling inside of these
heavenly veins—my adrenaline racing.
Knowing that my aunt does love me best than most
all the world is a sentimental virtue.
She is the sweetest brine of the rushing oceans of this heart.
Is it not she who has made this child a woman of
fervor with worldly passion?
Was it not the hem of her queenly robes that I held en route to the
throne room of GOD?
By aromatic winds from the most perfumed bouquet
of scattered roses from seaside,
I speak with vigor her warm name by the taste of my hallway telephone.
Is it really Mrs. Shamberger, the sister of my loving mommy?
Is this not my holy aunt who has led me
from the strong-bondaged cities?
Did she not cry hot tears of compassion as she watched me
drop to my knees and repent?
Lord, yes, this lady called Mildred is the
cherished esquire of the rest of my life,
and if ever I fail to let her know that I love her with
every atom of my every membrane
then may I be thus forgiven by my jealous GOD.
Now as the most unsweetest part of the night prevails,
we whisper goodbye in vain.
Gearing my receiver to holder, I kiss bye,
blue candle flames—my heart still burns for her.

Fools Gold

She loved in the image of the Quiet star
she's finally come to be
or the cherubic pats of winter rain
on the mist above the sea.
Now blood to blood our fingers touched
under the Baltimore Harbor moon,
and we became best friends for life
a "for life" that came so soon.
Oh, much too much, she loved a man
as holy as it seems,
and much too much, he loved in vain
all pastures glazed with green.
Now timidlike, my sister dwells
in the pampered rays of death.
A fool to see the worth in love
immune to precious breath.
Residuals of her life still glare
beneath the ocean's foam.
I'll see her when my day is done
and the rapture calls me home.

KINGS WITHOUT THRONES

Like GOD of my GOD, he reigns from the portrayal
of a whitewashed throne,
deciding my fate in his tainted little world.
My future, it's resting at the ball of his pen,
and the prevaricating lips of a lady friend.
We just don't bleve you can handle this job
spills from his mouth or his lust to be king.
Yet no less do I feel my efforts in vain,
the sweat of my blood or the pain of my pain.
Still I soothe fat ankles that killed to be best.
Feet calloused and blistered to please his highness.
Five minutes he lived in this lady's strife
then decided my fate for the rest of my life.
I curse the black pen that coursed through my heart,
and the polished baal fists that pushed it apart.
The dazzling bright dreams of this lady stands tarnished
—the ink from his pen has scraped off the varnish.
And do I know that a king must be king to be king.
So tonight I'll eat cheese by the throne of this thing,
I'll have my night cheese by the throne of that man,
not by the timid pen of a withering hand.

Rape by Candlelight

(A dedication to all my precious readers)

In the infant hours of water-impersonated days, there is a
personification of wetness.
Why do we give it the clean characteristic of the morning dews,
as it is no less the rain?
Still contentedly I squat by the windowside, weaved basket in lap,
peeling sweet onions that cannot make me cry, that defeats the purpose
of what they are meant by nature to be.
Through sugared perfection, are they no less strong fruit that
compliment temples of God?
In the terroristic threat of storms by the dimness of dusk
and beige crying sky, I can feel.
I feel the onion tips that blow from my apron skirt as
I cook by flickering electric light.
Small and sizzling tremors of unbusy currents rush
through my soft flesh with heaving.
As called by man, it is static from a clinging curtain,
as called by the host . . . shock?
To common philosophy, it is thus a symbol of life;
to the tremored, it is a token of pain.
Need I be so bold as to tell the world of the interruption
of time that erases breathing.
As told by many, we will sleep. As told by reality,
we will cease to live . . . we will die.
We see what we will, when we will, how we will,
and under the sweetest possible alias.
Need I be so frank in tongue as to tell the world
the truth of the sharp stinging bumblebees
with sticks so like a Junior Hitler—who dared
pour the sweetest honey over their noses.

YOUR NAME WILL TAKE YOU TO ANOTHER LEVEL

On a seasoned night in midevening,
I stopped past your circle of heaven called church.
Oiled chariots called feet, intact, head bent from the fine
French kisses of winter in spring.
Step by sensitive step, I pondered through shrouds
upon shrouds of mystic March crickets
through the church doors I danced to hear you preach
for our absent pastor this fine night.
From each chamber of my philosophical heart,
I could smell sizzling warmth of a sermon.
Fresh it was alive-as-Southern-white-linen on
mohair ropes in spring that cries as willows.
Still, it was no time for me to pray in the china berry squares
of lampless cities up north.
Just no more time to polish the leaping wick of my
oil-rinsed Christian light before men.
No time to taste the sweet tea in unprofitable waters of
Eve's fruit on my scorched tongue.
Somewhere inside the petrified temples of my
own swelled chest, there had been rest.
There had been a proudness for the love of my first
God—without the conviction of idols.
Now, who am I? The lady that lives between
Cinderella slippers and parliament hat?
Breezing through a pulsating troposphere that soft night,
armlocked with Satan, I came
to hear you speak to an audience of three.
I sank to white bench or the belly of the whale.
Within clouds upon clouds of white crickets at
my washed feet, I stood sleepy-tongued.

Under the glittering and perfumed chandeliers of heaven,
I smiled as you got to your car
with a loving family about you, and not once
did you look back to taste my inspiration.
Your unvoided words rose me to another level,
beyond parched berry trees, beyond prayer.

Inspired by Minister G. Warren Thompson

ONLY FOOLS STILL BREATHE

Maybe I no longer hold the midnight in the gray deep
of natural hair that no more shines,
and just maybe it ain't so thick as in yesterday, but it grows.
Now maybe my baby brown eyes are bluing
in fidgety skin moving without movement,
and just maybe my faltering vision is fading like dustlight,
but I see you still.
Just maybe these here soft female fingers are crimping
in arthritic pain as I write
with a diabetic tingle at the base of my tips, but still I sign my checks.
Oh, maybe once-white enameled teeth that used to
click in cold are dancing much more,
and maybe my fresh breath has tainted,
but my sandwich still tastes good.
Now I watch you by the party-lit shores of
an evening sea here at the beach of my youth.
Gumming pudding bowls in palms, you walk to see if I still know you.
Now I smell your exquisite European perfume,
the same as, but much sweeter than mine.
as you walk toward the seasoned winds of fall, and I still breathe.
Now I wink a fresh eye at the young guy next to me
that handed me my dropped cane,
and he frowns an *ugh* that once was a shy grin of desire,
but I think that I love him.
And now I wobble from the scene of the crime
with age-old guilt in my youthless bones,
and the cops suspect me not, just helps me across the street,
but I still did it.
Oh, maybe my mind is doggy with ideas of my day
as nostalgia sets in unsure as the sun.
Oh, how I long and I drool for the day of my young youth.
Oh, how I hate it when you measure my coffin size and
nod for the presence of my spirit.

Oh, you of no faith in me, I want to live. I want to live.
No there is no shame in breathing the breaths
afforded by an only God in a world by God.
Should I grab my new novel and just wait to die?
Through the Peter Principle of time I will not,
foolishly rise to the level of my demise.
By mercy of God and traitorous time, I will become ripe
with youthful old age.

TAKING THE WATER OUT OF PURE RAIN

If I am to hate, I am to legally come to grips
with the meaning of love in reverse.
So now, I watch you through the European vapors of my
Earl Grey tea, and I know you.
All cigarettes butted and soda cans firm on coasters,
the real world is surfaced nearby.
Woman, have you not the melancholy face of a tyrant
I once knew in my godly youth?
And will I not run from you as I did run from
temptation in my most tempting day?
Will you ever see that I cascade and breathe
with love for you inside a ring of fiery hate?
I hate you with fury, but my life I lay down for you
on any hot and cloudy day or Sunday.
Oh, woman, so far from my so-called evil eyes,
your friend would have bit you by now.
Does he not hate with, not much, but just a little bit of
death in his chilled veins?
Through the foggy fires of Saint Elmo, I ask just how
much death does it take to die?
Oh, you so close to my so-called smile, we live our
borrowed lives pretending to live
and never walking the fine lines between love and hate
on light spectrums not really here.
Now, if you are to hate than you are to come
to reality with the meaning of affection.
So now, I just watch you beyond the anointed
white ribbons in my biblical book of God.
All candle flames kindled and cooking pots smothered,
the real world is about to surface.

Woman, have you not the promise of a waterless rain in
Seattle through my hating eyes?
When every drip pocket in life is powdery dry,
whose love will alter your thirst for love?
My warm heart or the cat that smiles six feet above
you with the canary in his belly?

KINGS BENEATH KINGS

Somewhat the communist mists of little Everest
is lower than the planes of your feet
But darkness fell upon you as sin fell upon
the dirty fruit grids inside the gums of Adam
You walk politically as a man sugaring his berries
with the blood of the dammed.
Now in the arenas of smoky May rains
I can hear pats of dew on your parliament hat.

As I watch your burned chariots flashing white mustangs
on the altars of your corners,
And I sit in warmth, in holy captivity, the benches of Methuselah; I can smell your youth.
In my hot P cap, irons of mildewed life drip from my painted brows as Noah's clean rain
And you come across like the potted fog horns that treaded icy cracks of pharaoh's Red Sea.

You smile an unintimidated smile across the plateaus
of your insinuating chin
But still, I know you by the pores of your pocketbooks
when they're broke as the Titanic.
I know you by inner-city bops of rich strides that you use
to walk like Enoch with GOD.
And I'll know you when you suck for breath upon
the blue-washed liver of Jonah's whale.

Now that the mists of little Everest is beneath the shrouds
of your confederate new feet
You stand low upon the monopolized threshold of failure
to fail in a land built by utopia.
By the rolling sweat of God's hand, you have been picked
like the peppers of Peter Piper,
Never again may your proud and regal corsets bow lower
to any king lower than a king!

From *Angels Without Wings*

Fool of the Harbor

"I don't like fat people, do you?" That is what the ad said. Corey found it stuck to the side of his chair as his younger sister, Lisa, rode him away from the circus, which they had enjoyed just moments earlier. Where had this ad come? The wind must have blown it over to me while I was laughing at the clowns. But why did it come to me? Corey wondered. I am certainly not fat.

Corey pulled a small looking glass from the pocket of his blue windbreaker. He stared back cheerfully at the ten-year-old boy who looked back at him. He certainly did not see a fat person. Instead, he saw a handsome young boy with pretty brown eyes, light black hair, and a strong peaches-and-cream complexion, who was riding down the crowded downtown Baltimore streets in his wheelchair.

Just as Corey was sticking the mirror back into his pocket, the mean October wind blew one big whoosh and sucked the ad from his clutching fingers. "Get it, Lisa!" yelled Corey, startling his sister, who had not even noticed the ad until now. Corey knew that he could not go after the ad. Because of cerebral palsy, his body was too stiff to move around a lot, but he certainly did know how to show Lisa which direction to go.

"You are going the wrong way!" yelled Corey, as Lisa chased a small piece of foreign paper that she thought was the ad. Meanwhile, the little ad soared higher, higher, higher, and then higher. It must have gotten tired because it suddenly wriggled and floated until it landed right on the end of Lisa's cute little nose.

"What is this thing?" exclaimed Lisa, snatching up the tiny ad and flipping it over.

"You're nine years old," said Corey. "You can read." Lisa pinched the ad between her thumb and index finger, and read out loud, "I am too fat. I need help losing weight. For two free poodles, can you help my scale to say that I am lighter? If so, come by 77A Creamcake Way." Corey was surprised. He had not seen an address in the ad before Lisa read it. It must have been on the back.

"Come on," said Corey, "we must hurry home. It is starting to get dark." Cory and Lisa went two blocks down the street to their small home opposite the Inner Harbor, a popular tourist attraction in Baltimore.

That night, Corey could not sleep. He tossed and turned and kept thinking about those two free poodles.

He had always wanted a poodle, but his dad said they cost too much. Who was this mystery person who wanted to be thin, and how could he help him or her?

Well, he would find out tomorrow when he paid them a visit. Corey thought so long and hard about this fat person that before he knew it, the Saturday morning sun was beaming down on his thick black lashes.

"Lisa, Lisa," yelled Corey to the room across the hall, "I've decided to try my luck."

Lisa knew Corey so well that she did not even bother to ask him what he meant. It was already understood. Besides, she was proud that her big brother was claimed by many to be the smartest guy in

Harbor Place where they lived. He knew what he was doing. Lisa was already dressed as she yelled back, "Well, let's go. I'm excited about it too."

Corey and Lisa entered the long and cemented driveway of 77A Creamcake Way. They approached a beautiful cobblestone home, which smelled of candy apples and hot chicken soup. A fat tiger-striped cat sat on the front steps, nodding sleepily, and a plump, round girl, around ten or eleven years old, with glossy cheeks answered the door.

"Don't tell me, let me guess," said the plump girl as she motioned for Corey and Lisa to enter the huge elegant home with crystal chandeliers and a snow white carpet. "You are here to answer my twin brother's ad."

At that moment, Corey noticed a long line of children standing in front of someone. Each of them held a small strip of paper like what Corey had found when he was leaving the circus. In that line were fat children, skinny children, short children, and tall children. Some children were dressed up in funny clothes, some were well dressed while others were poorly dressed.

"Wow," said Lisa, looking bewildered, "everyone wants two free poodles."

"Let's go," said Corey, looking disillusioned and dropping his head. "We don't stand a chance. There are just too many children here."

Corey knew right then that the poodles belonged to some other child in the crowd. As he and Lisa headed for the front door, Corey heard his name called by a hoarse and strange voice, "Corey, Corey." He glanced around. The crowd had moved back some and Corey could see a fat, round little boy sitting at the front of the line in a beautiful black cashmere recliner, licking a shiny red lollipop.

"Glad you could make it," said the boy. "I have been hearing some very ugly rumors about you."

"Like what?" said Corey inquisitively.

"I hear that you are supposed to be the wizard of your neighborhood," said the boy sarcastically.

"Well, I have been known to solve many a problem for friends and acquaintances," said Corey proudly. It was true. Corey knew that the children in his neighborhood called him a genius, but even a genius could not show this boy how to get thin. He was way too fat! In fact, the boy was so fat that his stomach looked like a huge beach ball, covered with cloth, sitting in his lap.

"What do you suggest?" said the boy, lifting a pudgy hand to his mouth to take a big lick from his sucker while pointing to his big stomach with the other hand. Corey was at a loss for words as every eye in the room watched him intently. He remained silent.

"That's what I thought," said the boy, now laughing at Corey. Every child in the room began laughing wildly and pointing at Corey.

"You should not have even shown up," yelled a voice from inside the crowd of laughter. "You should not be known as the genius of Harbor Place. You should be called the 'Fool of the Harbor.'"

Another voice yelled, "Hey, Corey, how much is one plus one? You might want to count on your fingers if you even know how to count." The laughter got so loud it rang out in the air.

"What ideas have any of you come up with?" asked

Lisa defensively as she watched her brother lower his head.

"Well," said a tall slim boy dressed in a blue-jean set, "I suggested that he drink sixteen gallons of water while standing on his left elbow."

Another voice yelled, "That is absurd. He should take all of his meals in the middle of the ocean while on a boat to downtown Mexico." Before long, almost every child in the room had given some strange method for the fat boy to lose weight.

"Well," said Fat Boy, looking puzzled, "I guess a genius is someone who can fix any problem."

"Well," said Corey, "I am indeed a fool, but please know that a fool is merely a genius turned inside out. I will prove how big of a fool I really am by flipping myself inside out. Have you read your own ad?" asked Corey.

"Don't be silly. Of course I have," retorted Fat Boy.

"I wrote it."

"Are you a person of your word?" asked Corey.

"Just get on with it," said Fat Boy in an irritated and impatient voice.

"Sure," said Corey picking up the beautiful white pearl-like scale sitting on the floor next to Fat Boy's recliner. Lisa helped him open up the scale, place a device in it, close it, and return it to the floor. Everyone stared open-mouthed and inquisitively. Just what was he supposed to be doing?

"Okay, now stand on it," said Corey smiling proudly.

"No!" said Fat Boy. "You have done nothing to make me lose weight. There were no diets, exercise, or alterations involved in any manner. The only way that my scale could say that I am lighter is if you adjusted it, which you obviously did."

"Well," said Corey, "look at it. Do you see an adjustment? When you stand on it, if it reads that your weight is even one pound under your normal weight, then you will know that it has been tampered with."

Fat Boy was smiling again now. "Still, if it does not say that I weigh less, I get to keep my poodles," he said.

"I know," said Corey. "It must say that you are lighter while your normal weight is not to change at all."

"We all know that's impossible," said Fat Boy as he rolled to his right side, stood up, and bounced his full weight down on the little scale. How could his scale possibly say that he weighed less without changing his actual weight? Fat Boy was even more convinced now that Corey really was a big fool. Then it happened.

Just as Fat Boy's feet touched the scale and it rolled over to his usual one hundred and fifty pounds, he was startled by a muffled sound. The sound became clearer. It said the words, "That I am lighter." It repeated these words over and over again until Fat Boy stepped off of the scale, looking bewildered and surprised.

Corey had placed a small tape recorder inside the scale that spoke the words "That I am lighter" whenever it was activated by someone stepping on it.

Corey had made the scale do just as Fat Boy had asked in his ad. The ad said Fat Boy wanted his scale to say "That I am lighter." He never once asked to lose weight. Fat Boy picked up his ad read it, then looked at Corey.

"What do you know?" yelled a crowd member. "We were the ones who did not understand the ad. Fat Boy was not trying to lose weight, he merely asked that we make his scale say 'That I am lighter.'" The children began to cheer wildly for Corey and Lisa.

"You are indeed a fool turned inside out, Corey," said the fat boy. "You have discovered my secret message. You asked if I were a person of my word.

Well, answer your own question, Mr. Genius," he said, placing two radiant white fluffy, baby poodles on Corey's lap. "Oh, by the way, my name is Kevin," said Fat Boy.

Everyone laughed as they left the Creamcake Way home, singing heroic tunes to the genius of the Harbor Place.

A Vampire Lives Upstairs

Whoever said that vampires did not exist had never met Ms. Abby. I slouched lazily on the dingy white front steps of my Memorial Street home located in Northwest, Washington DC The calm and serene September 1967 winds softly breathed small electric fizzes of mist and dusk dew across my young brown cheeks. Never in my entire eleven years of life had I ever dreamed I would be the one to prove the existence of those foul, tainted creatures—vampires!

I innocently rubbed my sweaty palms up the length of my blue tip tennis shoes, faded blue wranglers, white sweatshirt, and black pageboy hair. Although it was quite cool outside, bouncing kernels of sweat leaped to the surface of my forehead like popping popcorn as I watched Mama standing next door, talking to our neighbor, Ms. Abby.

Ms. Abby must have been well over one hundred years old with her crumpled raisin-brown skin, crooked nose, long sharp, canine teeth, tall skinny frame, and humped back. She had waist-length, dull straggling ivory-white hair and smelled eerily like medieval mothballs. She had extra long clawlike black fingernails that seemed to somehow glow in the dark. I stared at Ms. Abby for what seemed like hours inside of minutes while she stood there in her long ankle-length black funeral dress. Her dress rested over thick black orthopedic boot-shoes.

Why was she talking to my mother, and what were they whispering about? We had lived next door to Ms. Abby for six months now, and she never usually said anything more to us than "Hi." There was something strange and creepy about Ms. Abby. I just could not put my finger on it at the time, but I soon found out what it was. Ms. Abby was indeed a vampire, and I was terrified of her.

I could almost feel her gray boiled-fish eyes on me as I watched Mama and her talk ever so softly, underneath their girlish giggles, and the soft spraying Northern rain. Oh, why did we ever move into that neighborhood? All houses in the block were identical, all gray three-story buildings that creaked and reeked with age. Give or take a few tombstones here and there, and our little neighborhood would have been complete.

Ms. Abby's house was the oldest on the block and was covered with dead vines that seemed to live forever from her cellar windows to her chimney top.

There were so many dead trees on our block that it was virtually impossible for the sunlight to reach us.

On cloudy days, the city had to turn on dim yellow streetlights for us in the daytime as well as at night.

We dwelled in a quiet spooky area, and living next door to Ms. Abby did not help one bit.

I was so afraid of Ms. Abby that I hated walking past her door. I would walk an entire block in the opposite direction just to get to the corner candy store next door to Ms. Abby in order to spend my nickels at the candy shop. The last time that I passed Ms.

Abby's house, she had this huge oblong mirror attached to her door. It looked strange, and I hated it.

By this time, I was so engrossed in thought that I did not hear my brave fourteen-year-old sister, Bev, walk up behind me. I always admired Bev. She was like an iron girl. She was strong, fearless, rational, and calm.

Nothing could scare her, or so we all thought.

In the middle of my thoughts, it happened! My biggest fears came to the surface. I suddenly saw Ms. Abby step back as she laughed with Mama. I felt a hot rush of heat possess my entire body as I glared from a side view at the mirror on Ms. Abby's door. She stood directly in front of it, yet it did not cast a reflection. I was flabbergasted.

Just as I was about to yell for Mama, I heard her laughing voice say, "Go into the house with Bev."

"It's getting dark out here, and I have to leave for a moment." I couldn't believe what I was seeing.

Ms. Abby actually fixed her scary gray eyes on me as my mother entered that house with her.

No! She could not have gone in. This could not be happening. Ms. Abby took a tattered old, wrinkled thumb, rubbed it across her bleeding red teeth, and laughed while looking at me as she entered the door with Mama. I was virtually on fire with perspiration now as I leaped to my feet in fear. She was planning to bite Mama and make her a vampire too. At that point, my mom and the vampire completely disappeared inside the musty old dwelling.

I screamed "Oh no!" and began to run toward that much-feared house. I had to get Mama out of there before she was bitten. Suddenly and somewhere inside the thick settling fog and night spray, I felt a strong warm hand clasp my wrist as I approached Ms. Abby's front steps. It was Bev's voice saying, "Oh no, you don't. You stay away from that house."

"Are you crazy?" I yelled almost in tears. "She is going to bite our mother. We have to save her." I felt like gallons upon gallons of blood rush to my head as I desperately sobbed.

"Didn't you see her rub her bleeding teeth as they went into the house?" I exclaimed.

Bev, for the first time, looked puzzled and uncertain as she finally said, "Okay you may go in, but we will sneak in together. I will show you once and for all that there is no such thing as vampires!"

I watched Bev's slender brown fingers grasp the opening of Ms. Abby's gray peeling door, which was slightly ajar as her faded blue wranglers and powder blue sweatshirt disappeared inside. Naturally, I followed.

Although I did not realize it at the time, after this night, I would never again be able to call my brave sister fearless again. As I quietly tiptoed inside the vampire's house to rescue my mother, I felt an icy rush of wind out of nowhere sweep over my entire body. I shivered with fear. The house was cold, drafty, damp, and musty. The living room was bare except for the cracked, molded gray cement walls, a splinter-filled old wooden floor, a smelly antiquated black leather couch, and a rusty old kerosene lamp sitting on the floor by the dining room entrance, flickering wildly. The house smelled of a mixture of earth, warm blood, and stale roasted nuts.

As Bev and I broke through thick spider webs and flying dust to enter the rest of the house, I clutched my crumpled brown vampire bag tighter. I had created it for protection when I first learned that Ms. Abby was part of the lurking undead. My bag contained a huge brass cross, a small jar of garlic salt, two small brown plastic stakes that I had made from the legs of my toy tea set table, a small spice container containing faucet water which I had blessed myself, and a yellow crayon marked Sunlight. I kept it with me wherever I went.

No vampire could bite me as long as I had it, at least that is what I thought until Bev and I reached the entrance to Ms. Abby's dining room.

We could not see through the dark dining room fog, but we could certainly hear through it. There was a loud sudden *Pop*! The house became pitch-black. I felt an overwhelming hot flush rush to my head as goose bumps began to crawl and leap all over the surface of my skin. I trembled in fear as I turned to run back out of the front door. Through the darkness, I heard Bev's voice pseudo-calmly say, "Don't be afraid, Lynne, I'm sure there is a logical explanation for all of . . ."I did not even stay to hear the rest of Bev's sentence. I fled for the door in terror. Before I reached the front door, I suddenly heard Mama's loud shrill scream pierce the mystic blackness. I felt lightheaded, and quite faint now. It did not take a brick wall to tumble down on my head for me to figure out that Ms. Abby had just bitten Mama and was on her way to Bev and me.

I could feel her eerie tainted presence creeping toward us and shadowing us as if in slow motion with the authority of a fake god. We were doomed. Out of nowhere, I heard Ms. Abby's spooky voice amplified through the air with a horrible, bone-chilling echo.

"One down and two to go," she snickered hoarsely.

With a freezing cold human body trailing closely behind me, I finally reached the front door. Grasping the knob of the just-entered door, I yanked, pulled, kicked, and screamed. The door had slammed shut behind Bev and me and would not reopen. My heart pounded so hard that I was quite sure it would rip through my chest at any second. My body went limp, weak, hot, and then cold with fear and fever.

My mother was now a vampire, and Bev and I were trapped and about to become vampires as soon as Ms. Abby bit us, which she would surely do. I fought and struggled with the door furiously as I listened to Bev's shaky voice yell in terror, "LYNNE, YOU WERE Right. Help! Let's get outta here!"

Bev was terrified. I felt the salty tears trickle down my moist cheeks as I waited in fear for the inevitable and continued to struggle. Then it happened! I felt a rough, clammy, clawlike hand grasp the hot, moist flesh of my forearm. Bev and I quickly screamed in raging fear. Two sharp, simultaneous, painless stabs on the right side of my neck complemented the hand grasp. I was flabbergasted. I had just been bitten!

Just as I felt the warm liquid ooze down from my neck wounds, the door that I was struggling with clicked and opened. I was in a semistate of shock. I did not know which way to run. I was no longer human and had, therefore, lost all of my ability to reason as an average eleven-year-old girl. I was now a vampire. Had someone told me that I would become a vampire this night fifteen minutes earlier, I would not have ever believed it.

Upset and disoriented, I ran aimlessly out of Ms. Abby's front door with Bev on my heels. I felt wild and bewildered. Now, just where should a fresh young vampire run for help? I had read so many vampire books and watched hundreds of vampire movies yet had no idea what to do next.

Just as I was about to break down sobbing, I suddenly and instinctively looked up at Ms. Abby's front door. Big as my past life, there was her door mirror. Bev and I were standing directly in front of it about to run, yet we were casting no reflection in it.

Just as I felt my knees loosen and buckle under me in preparation to faint, Ms. Abby's front door creaked open further, and she and Mama stepped out, casually laughing their same casual and girlish laughter.

"I heard you two girls come in," laughed Ms. Abby, easily picking homemade red taffy candy from her long dull teeth. Bev was staring at Ms. Abby blankly as if she were a ghost instead of a vampire.

"Hey, Lynne," said Ms. Abby, "you girls should have seen it. I invited your mom inside to sample some of the treats that I am preparing for the fall carnival this year. Anyway," laughed Ms. Abby, "I had a sudden power outage. For some reason, I always get three short outages per month, and they always occur one behind the other. Anyway, it scared my pet mouse, Rusty. He leaped across your mom's feet in the dark, causing her to scream in fear."

I desperately searched the contours of her wrinkled face for the slightest hint of a lie. There was none to be found.

Ms. Abby continued to talk. "Hey, Lynne, didn't ya feel me grab your arm in the vestibule? I was trying to warn you about those two plastic sticks that had busted through your little bag here," she said calmly, dangling my little brown vampire bag in the air.

"Oh look, you've gone and stuck yourself in the neck with those sticks too."

She carefully peered at the two small wounds on the right side of my neck. I had forgotten that I was still holding my vampire bag while I was trying to get the front door open. Ms. Abby then looked at the mirror on her door, and said to Mama, "I really need a new place to live. My electricity fails, my door sticks, and this ole trick mirror that I put on my door couldn't scare away a vampire."

She gently shoved two small white storage bowls into Mama's hands. One contained dry roasted nuts, and the other one contained some sort of red taffy.

"Tell me how you all like it," she said to my mother.

They both smiled at each other, said goodnight, and walked toward their doors.

Still puzzled as to what was really going on, I wiped the splashed homemade holy water from my neck and began walking with Mama and Bev toward the house.

Bev looked at me and whispered, "Well, you see, Lynne, Ms. Abby had us both fooled. A vampire does live, but not in Ms. Abby's house."

Confused and happy about not being a vampire, I looked at her once again. I was puzzled. "Then where does it live?" I asked inquisitively.

Bev put a forefinger on the crown of my head and said, "A vampire lives upstairs."

I did not understand her at the time, but years later, when I was all grown-up, I realized that she was right.

A vampire did indeed live upstairs, and I could only bring it out through my own imagination. The real vampire did exist but solely in my own mind.

The Fifteenth Key

"Read this line and die! That's right, you will die laughing. This site is hilarious!" Those were the bold black Ariel fonts spread across the Windows 95 computer screen. James stood arms folded in his bedroom, admiring his computer screen. Christmas of '96 had proven to be the best yet for him. He finally had the Internet. What more could a thirteen-year-old eighth-grader ask? James looked around at his glossy radiant walls made of the finest mirrors that Washington DC had to offer. Snickering lightly, he curled his bare toes around strands of clean soft white pellets of wall-to-wall semishag carpet which complemented thick white floor-length drapes. The drapes faced his beautiful king-sized, satin-covered, canopy, feather bed. He had it all—a 1921-style black-and-white dresser/nightstand set, a black Oriental phone sitting on the nightstand next to his bed, and a fifty-inch-screen television set with a double-deck VCR facing his bed. James rested a content elbow on his 1995 black stereo equipment. He took a deep breath, inhaling the aroma of his dinner being cooked. It smelled like garlic scampi and fresh banana pudding. Sitting down in his keyboard and clicking onto the wrestling gossip Web site, he learned that his favorite wrestler, Dynamite Dinos Davis, would win the world title in the near future, and his least favorite wrestler, Andreo "the Fly Super Guy" Brown would lose a career match to the amazing one—Shawnt Trapp. Just as James was about to read the next rumor, he was interrupted by a loud booming noise followed by their maid, Ms. Beverly's voice. She was always so bossy when his politician parents were away on business. He and his sister, Kimberly, could have little or no fun.

"Hold it! Hold it!" yelled Ms. Beverly's hoarse Southern voice. "I ain't gonna have dat running up them stairs while I'm in charge. You boeys wanna see James, you betta act like propa young min."

Through casual snickers and pseudo-silence, James could hear "yes, ma'am's" and "sorrys." Before he could get up, the door to his room burst open and in popped Tavon, Barry, and Trevor—his three best friends and classmates. With them was another young man who looked rather mysterious. The new boy looked to be around twelve or thirteen. He wore black jeans and a sweatshirt just like James and his friends who liked to dress alike, and he wore a long silver brace on his left leg. James could not help noticing that the dark complected boy had lime-green eyes. Is that what made him look so weird? The boys gathered around the computer, hands in pockets, staring in awe at the screen.

"Wow," sighed Tavon, "I can't believe it. You finally got the Internet. James Edmund Vines can explore new lines."

This remark caused a roar of laughter. James hopped up from his chair, reached out a small hand to the strange-looking boy, and said, "Hi, I am James Edmund Vines. Who are you?"

The boy looked puzzled as he reached down to shake James's hand. "My real name is Dajaun Davon Kelly. I'm thirteen years old, and everybody calls me Wizzy cause I'm real smart, 'specially when it comes to the Internet." He handed James a wrapperless stick of mint gum. "We all got mint gum," said Wizzy. The boys began to pop and smack gum as if in agreement.

"I live in Annapolis, Maryland," said Wizzy proudly. "I'm here in DC visiting my cousin, Barry, during the Christmas vacation." He nodded at Barry who instinctively nodded back. Wizzy leaned his head to one side and said casually, "Hey man, why you so short?"

"I ain't short," said James, popping the piece of mint gum in his mouth. James had forgotten that he had dwarfism, a growth disorder that only allowed him to grow to three feet and nine inches. No one had mentioned his dwarfism in a long time. This guy was really weird.

"I got dwarfism," said James.

"Oh," said Wizzy as if he actually knew what dwarfism was. "How come your sister is tall?" he asked, shrugging.

"I dunno," said James. "Probably 'cause she's fourteen."

The boys started to laugh and punch keys on the computer.

"Move over," said Wizzy, sticking out his chest proudly. "Let a true genius in." Laughing, the other boys moved aside.

"Watch this," said Barry wide-eyed and excited.

"He can sho-nuff work this thing."

"*Phooey*," said James as if he were unimpressed.

"I work the Internet all the time in school just like you guys. We know the Internet real well too."

"*SSSSHH*," said Trevor excitedly, "not like Wizzy, watch, James."

Wizzy eased down into James's chair and began to work the keyboard with the confidence of Beethoven sitting at a priceless piano. The boys watched excitedly as Wizzy entered a pretty mint-green gypsy Web site.

"Why did you go there, Wizzy?" asked Trevor. "We ain't interested in no gypsies, we jest wanna see some games or sports, man."

Wizzy looked quite puzzled. Instead of answering, he continued to punch the keyboard. For some reason, the mint-green screen would not vanish. Wizzy pounded the keys even harder. But the screen remained unchanged.

"Here, let me," said James, crawling under Wizzy's arm to get to the keyboard. "This computer is just used to my touch." The boys snickered as James began to punch the keys. Not one of them suspected that an eerie mystery was concealed behind that green screen.

The boys took turns attempting to make the screen disappear. After about twenty minutes, James decided to just leave it and try again later. Just as the boys began to slowly move away from the computer screen, it happened. The entire screen went dark green, and a caption danced gracefully across the screen in big bold letters: Gypsy Lovers At My Site, I Grant You Each One Wish Tonight, Click On These Words.

"Hey, let's try it," said Barry, running back to the screen. The boys became very excited with the exception of Wizzy. Wizzy sat down calmly in James's chair and stared inquisitively at the computer screen.

"Don't do it, guys," said Wizzy quietly. "I smell a rat. I don't know what it is just yet, but I think it would be a big mistake to find out."

"Yeah, right," said Barry cynically. "You don't know everything, Wizzy." The other boys let out a lot of "yeahs" and "that's right."

"Okay," yelled Wizzy, throwing up his hands in surrender. "I will do it first." Wizzy placed a trembling finger on the word "Click" and pushed. The screen stayed green and the words "Place Wish One Here" appeared in place of the previous instructions.

"Speak into the mike, Wizzy," said James, handing Wizzy the microphone to his computer.

"You ain't supposed to wish out loud," Tavon stammered as if he were asking a question instead of making a statement.

"Well, you have to," said Wizzy. "Much as we would like to think so, computers ain't human. They can't read minds. Now I need quiet so I can make a wish." Wizzy clutched the microphone tightly as if it were trying to escape from him and then casually leaned forward and spoke into it.

"I wish," said Wizzy, "that whatever mystery lives behind this screen will reveal itself, then leave us alone." Tavon, Barry, and Trevor snickered.

"Hey, you guys have no right to laugh at someone's wish," said James angrily. "We all have the right to wish whatever we want. If Wizzy chooses to believe that there is something scary behind this screen, let him. Who gets hurt from it?"

In the midst of fading smiles, Tavon traded places with Wizzy and spoke into the microphone.

"I wish to have so much education that I never have to go to school again," said Tavon matter-of-factly.

All the boys began laughing.

"Watch out, Einstein," said Barry. "Let Mr. Barry show you guys what a real wish is like." Reaching for the microphone, Barry spoke slowly. "I . . . I would like to eat hot dogs nonstop." It was no secret that Barry's favorite food was hot dogs.

"Yeah, with plenty of mustard," added Trevor, sitting down and scooping up the microphone. "Hey, man," Trevor yelled into the microphone, "you probably know that I keep a penny bank in my bedroom. Right now, I got four dollars and nine cents. I wish that every penny in my room would never stop multiplying."

Handing James the microphone, Trevor stepped back.

James pursed his lips as he reached out for the microphone. He felt that every one of his friends knew what he would wish for. His thoughts were just too loud. If only he could think lower. But why should he?

His friends were going to hear his wish anyway. James wiped his mouth with the back of his fist. It did not take long for the words to push their way through his drawn lips. "I wish," said James uneasily as his gleaming eyes danced from one concerned face to another, "that she would come home." There was an eerie silence in the room, and then many warm hands on his shoulder.

"Let her rest," said Barry softly. "We all know how much it hurt you last Christmas, but it is over now.

Your grandma was a very sweet lady, and we all loved her, but she has a new kind of home now."

"You cannot possibly have your wish," said Trevor sympathetically.

"I know," said James sadly, dropping his head, "but dreams never hurt anyone."

At that precise moment, Ms. Beverly's dinner call slashed through the long, sad faces and pats on the back, breaking the spirit. "We better go now," said Tavon, motioning to the other boys.

After casual good-byes, a long, tedious supper, and helping Kimberly with the dinner dishes, James headed excitedly up to his room to get back on the Internet. Although he was certainly excited by the challenge of exploring different lines that awaited him on the Internet, James was not prepared for the fate that awaited him inside his room.

It happened so suddenly.

James felt an eerie, creepy sensation come over his entire body as he slowly pushed open the door to his room. He was stunned by the sharp, cold gust of wind that leaped out of his room, knocking him to his knees. James felt a sudden rush of hot and cold chills take over his now trembling body. Before he had a chance to stand up and run away, he felt his body being sucked inside the room against his will.

Torment ripped through him like a sword as he opened his mouth and tried to yell. What was happening to him? No sound would come out. Beads of perspiration leaped to the surface of his forehead as he felt his body being shoved into a chair by his window by a mystical force. Just as he was about to reach up and fight for his life, James caught a glimpse through his window of the two houses that faced his.

One was Trevor's and the other was Barry's. From where James had been pushed down, he could see clearly into the windows of their houses. It was not a pretty sight. James watched in awe as Trevor sat on his bed, counting pennies from his shiny pink penny bank. But something was wrong. Although the bank was no bigger than both of Trevor's hands put together, pennies kept popping out of the bank. Trevor was shaking it frantically as if he had no control over his actions. More and more pennies flew out from the little bank, spilling over onto the floor, bed, dressers, everywhere.

Soon James could see Trevor who, although he was surrounded by mountains of pennies, kept shaking his bank frantically,nonstop.

Somehow finding his voice, James began to yell wildly. No one came to his rescue. He continued to yell and wave his hands, trying to get Trevor to stop shaking the bank before he buried himself alive. But there was no response. Trevor was in a trancelike state and could not hear him. James began fighting harder to free his body from his invisible captor when through his window, he spied Barry sitting on his bed eating hot dogs, and Wizzy sitting in a trance at Barry's computer.

"Nooooo! Nooooo!" shouted James. Barry did not even notice him. James tried to lift his left arm to tap on the window and give a signal like he always did, but this time it was no-go. Then suddenly James's room went pitch-black, and out of nowhere, the overwhelming smell of a wet graveyard filled the air.

James ducked and shrieked in terror. What was happening to him? "Help! Help!" Still, no answer.

James watched in horror as Barry continued to shove raw hot dogs covered with plenty of mustard down his throat. James saw him double over as if in pain, but Barry continued to cough and shove more weenies, which appeared from out of nowhere into his open, waiting mouth. His body seemed to be getting more and more bloated, and he had a disgusted look on his face. Still, he continued as if in a trance.

As James made one final attempt to escape from the chair to which he was rooted, he noticed Tavon running up and down the block, yelling quotes from Shakespeare, Marx, and many other famous scholars.

He was screaming words James had never even heard before, he too was in a trancelike state. Why was no one helping them, and where was everyone?

James knew that he had to be strong. He felt a rush of strength as he finally wriggled free from the vicelike grip holding him in the chair. Just as he broke free and was about to run and help his friends, he felt his left foot curl under him. He fell flat on his back onto what used to be the floor. Attempting to push against the floor to get up, he grabbed up a handful of cemetery dirt and smelly broken tombstones. He screamed in fear and tried to get out of his bedroom door, which was jammed shut. Just as he whirled around in the darkness to find his crowbar, she appeared.

Through pitch-blackness and with the smell of earth, his grandmother's ghost appeared in a white, dirty gown, floating in midair, without feet! James went limp with fear. How much more could he take?

His grandmother's eyes were big as saucers as she stared straight at him. She began to laugh a shrill, piercing evil laugh. Her chilling laugh echoed through his room. A huge cold clawlike hand was just about to reach down and grab for him when James yelled, "Who are you? You are not my grandma!"

His grandmother had not been evil. She had been very kind and sweet. James suddenly and fearfully cried, "Be gone evil one!" James saw a big white flash and then his little room was back to normal.

James shivered and then heard his friends pounding on his door and screaming his name. Still sweating, trembling, and shaking, he ran to open it.

Tavon, Barry, Trevor, and Wizzy burst inside and began hugging each other as if they had not seen one another in years.

"What's up?" Wizzy said to James as he calmly walked over to the computer. "You look like you seen a ghost." Everyone stared, wide-eyed at Wizzy as he plopped down into James's computer chair and lifted a silver-braced leg onto the computer table.

Biting a stubby thumbnail, he leaned back, executive-style, and began to speak calmly, crisply, and wisely. "Now it is time for my wish," said Wizzy.

The boys searched Wizzy's lime-green eyes for the answer. "While you boys were receiving your wishes," explained Wizzy, "I had to sit at Barry's computer and search for my own wish. I reentered the gypsy Web site to find out what was going on and how it could be corrected."

Barry looked confused as he asked, "But how? I don't have the Internet."

"You did this evening," answered Wizzy without surprise.

"Because I had wished for the mystery behind the screen to reveal itself, and then leave us alone, it had to do so. It put me in a trance and showed me everything."

"What happened to us?" said Tavon inquisitively.

"Well, the reason that I made my wish was because when we were here the first time today, I noticed that James's e-mail address was to a local graveyard. I recognized it because a few months ago, my dad used to work the nightshift there. I used to e-mail him there sometimes."

Mouths dropped open in disbelief and awe.

"Why didn't you tell me?" asked James.

"Would you have believed me?" asked Wizzy calmly.

"No."

"Okay, then let me finish."

The boys were all ears as Wizzy continued. "Your e-mail address, James, first belonged to an evil gypsy descendant named Jan Mint. He was addicted to the Internet. He stayed on it night and day. For some odd reason, Mr. Mint stopped paying his Internet bill, and his service was cut off. Before he died, he vowed to get even with all of the companies who offered Internet service. Right now, every Windows 95 computer that has the Internet, or has ever had it, is cursed. Jan Mint has had his own Web page before his service was interrupted. He used to advertise good luck charms for sale on it. Anyhow, his curse went like this: any Windows 95 computer that has, or has ever had, the Internet has the curse of the fifteenth key."

"What's the fifteenth key?" asked all the boys together.

"Didn't ya know?" said Wizzy. "Anyone who hits the same key on their Internet Windows 95 computer while in the presence of Mint will be cursed forever by their own wishes. On the fifteenth time that a key is hit by anyone, the screen will appear, and if used, the users will be cursed after making their wishes."

"But how can we tell when we have hit the fifteenth key?" asked Barry.

"That's it," said Wizzy shrugging, "you can't tell. It can happen to anyone at any time. You wouldn't know unless you counted how many times you've hit each key."

"Well, what happens if you don't use the wishes when the screen appears?" asked Barry.

"You will still be cursed," said Wizzy. "You just won't know it."

"Did you hit Mint's cursed key fifteen times on James's keyboard?" asked Trevor.

"Oh no," said Wizzy, "James hit the cursed key fourteen times. I just punched the fifteenth key."

"Getting back to my story, whenever one of Mint's victims does not believe in the dreams that Mint sends to haunt them, the curse is lifted from that person forever. It can never bother that victim, or anyone who was in the trance with him again.

We'll assume that James was that disbeliever when he did not believe the ghost that he had seen was his grandmother," Wizzy finished.

James giggled. Everyone looked at him. Trying not to blush, James asked, "Why wouldn't anyone come to our rescue, Wizzy?"

"Because what happened to us never happened," said Wizzy shrugging. "It was the product of a sick dream. Other people can't see or hear someone else's dreams unless they are connected to that dream by some evil force. That evil force does not usually occur."

"Then we were all dreaming Mint's sick dreams," said James.

"That is correct," said Wizzy wisely. Everyone looked puzzled, except for Wizzy who pulled out and held up a stick of mint gum and said quietly, "While in the presence of Mint, we hit the fifteenth key."

They all laughed and unconsciously put everything behind them, including the Internet, which James decided to get rid of. It would probably be years before he and the Internet were ready for each other again.

Still, James secretly hoped that one day the rest of the world would learn about the curse of the fifteenth key.

I Can Still See the Angels

I am in love with Allae. Once, those soft exhilarating words had dominated my thoughts.

Christmas Eve of 1997 seemed to be turning into a nostalgic Christmas for me as I sat in front of my lovely white Christmas tree with my five-year-old daughter, Asa. Flashing radiant tree lights illuminated breathtaking silhouettes of tree ornaments on my living room walls and carpet. I could even see the shadows of snowflakes dancing and spinning on my easy chair and love seat.

A feeling of déjà vu began to creep into my mind as I set my mug of coconut chocolate on the coffee table and focused on the white drapes billowing out from the heat on the window behind my tree. No doubt, I had actually been down this route before, but when?

Where?

The faint crackling of the fireplace, in its own comfort zone, accented melodious strings of Christmas music. A light Texas rain rapped softly on my windowpane as if it were desperate to get in, away from itself.

Then it dawned on me. This Christmas scene was the same as one I'd lived twenty-eight years ago, with Mama and my three older sisters back home in Washington, DC. I was thirteen years old then. How could I ever have forgotten?

I watched the flashing tree in awe as the tree and its ornaments vanished inside of blackness every time the lights flashed off. All that could still be seen was a small band of six frosted angels dangling from the tree.

From inside the depths of flashing tree lights, I could hear Asa's young voice exclaiming, "Look, Mommy, we can still see the angels!"

Yes, that's right, I could still see the angels: Mama, my sixteen-year-old sister Bev, my fifteen-year-old sister Debbie, my fourteen-year-old sister Tandy, and me. We were all gathered around the decorated tree on

Christmas Eve of 1969, listening to Christmas music and talking about past Christmases.

Who was the sixth angel? His name was Allae Charlze Calvert. The first time I saw Allae was on thatChristmas Eve of 1969 when I was thirteen years old.

As Mama and we girls sat around the tree laughing, talking, drinking coconut chocolate, and listening to Christmas music, there was a light tap at the door. My rival and sister, Debbie, leaped energetically to her feet. "I will get it."

Out of Mama's four girls, Bev was known as the wisest, Debbie the most social, Tandy the most independent, and I was the prettiest. Still, my rival, Debbie, managed to capture the hearts of every young guy alive, or so it seemed to me. Secretly, I had begun to take interest in the opposite sex, only to see Debbie become the focus of the young men's attentions. Also secretly, I was a green-eyed monster when it came to Debbie. Just as Debbie reached the door, Mama said, "Debbie, you must ask who it is first."

Debbie carelessly yanked open the large wooden living room door. This was when I first saw Allae. He walked into my life out of the freezing, blowing December rain, dripping wet. I saw a tall, broad-shouldered guy with a pearly-white smile, olive-tan skin, and brown, shoulder-length and pony-tailed hair.

He was wearing a soaked white sweatshirt, wet blue jeans, and red-and-white Converse sneakers. He carried a red plastic shopping bag. Smiling, he nodded politely as he stamped his dripping feet on the welcome mat. As he entered, I could smell heavenly tropical cologne. It smelled of pineapples and lemons.

"You made it," said Mama, getting up to extend a soft plump hand.

"Everyone, this is Allae Charlze. He is sixteen years old and works with the Community Action Youth Committee at my job."

Allae sat his shopping bag next to Tandy's feet and smiled at Mama. "Sorry, it took me so long, Miss Rose," he said, "but I had to watch my twelve-year-old brother, Fred, until Mama and Dad got back from Christmas shopping. But, guess what? I brought you all gifts."

Allae pulled out boxes of all sizes, wrapped in green-and-red, holly-designed paper. Mama's box was the biggest. He began to hand the smaller boxes to the rest of us. He gave me a box, saying it was from the angels.

"Don't open 'em yet," said Bev, biting her bottom lip by habit and looking at Tandy, who was tugging at the red wrapping paper on her slim oblong box.

"That's right," said Mama, laughing along with Allae.

"It ain't Christmas yet."

Mama got up calmly and fished out our big box of emergency Christmas gifts for males. We always made up one box for males and one for females every Christmas, just in case we had to give gifts unexpectedly. Each of us began taking out gifts for Allae. I gave him a box containing a sterling silver wrist chain. I had wrapped it myself. As I handed Allae the box, our eyes met suddenly and our hands touched. I not only saw, but also felt his soft gray eyes resting on my young face. My entire face burned with hot-cold admiration. He was the handsomest and most soft—spoken guy I had ever encountered. I knew then that I was in love.

I watched Allae smiling, staring at me on and off, smiling for the next four hours. I knew then that he was in love with me as well. An overwhelming chemistry of mutual attraction intimately bloomed in the atmosphere between us; I felt confident that we both felt the vibes.

After the first hour or so, our hypnotic love trance was broken by Debbie slipping her long white robe over Allae's shoulders. "Please forgive our manners," Debbie said smiling at Allae. "You are still quite wet."

"Thank you, Debbie," Allae answered, now looking at her.

Holding tightly on my cup of coconut chocolate, it was all that I could do to hold back from dashing the entire contents into Debbie's round, flirting pie-face. I felt a strong surge of hate for her possess my entire body. I could clearly see that once again she too was attracted to Allae. I could not bear to know that.

I watched Debbie laugh and talk with Allae for the next two hours. I watched her yellow teeth break into wide grins as she batted her short skimpy lashes at him every time he said something amusing. To me, she laughed like she had a mouth full of runny Copenhagen snuff under her pushed-in pig snout of a nose. He could not possibly find her attractive. Tandy and I had nicknamed her "balloon gums." Even had she been pretty, I was not going to let her steal my Adonis from me.

But my Adonis eventually became my Judas when I watched Debbie walk down the aisle with him four years later at their wedding. For four years, I had watched Allae watching me while he courted my sister.

Still, he never treated me like anything but a little sister.

Could it be possible that he'd never really returned my love? As he lifted his right hand to take Debbie's hand at the reception, I could not help but notice the aged sterling silver arm-chain clinging to his wrist. Did he love me after all? He was still wearing my gift?

I watched that same silver chain dangle from Allae's wrist one year later as he sat in court signing the papers that freed him from Debbie's tainted clutches. The grounds were infidelity on Debbie's part.

I watched Debbie toss her head back as she glided out of the courtroom laughing, linked arm-in-arm with Gavin, her fourth boyfriend since her marriage to Allae.

While I was sitting in the courtroom, I removed from my purse the band of six frosted angels representing that fateful Christmas in 1969.

As my family left the courtroom teary-eyed, I clutched my six frosted angels tighter. The years had taught me that I'd never really loved Allae, but my childhood infatuation with him remained a sentimental attachment. My thoughts were broken by my new husband's voice.

"I don't know whether to leave with my old family or my new family," said my husband, Fred, jokingly.

Smiling, he waved goodbye to his brother, Allae.

It was a farewell wave that seemed to hearken back to the past because when Allae waved back with a bitter smile, our eyes met once again. Only this time, I saw only hurt and bitterness. Until I'd met Fred, I too had to endure the hurt of watching someone I thought I'd loved being stolen from me. Oh, how bad I felt for Allae. As our eyes met, something happened . . . The angels that I was clutching were still glowing after someone had dimmed the courtroom lights.

It was the same as the way that they still glowed in the darkness. As my Christmas lights flashed out, I could still see Allae's frosted angels glowing on my tree. I could still see his soft calm gray eyes. I could still hear his strong laughing voice. I could even smell every atom of his warm tropical cologne.

* * *

In 1974, several things happened. Allae divorced Debbie and joined the army-career status.

His brother, Fred, graduated from high school, married me, and joined the army for twenty years.

I later became a college instructor and now resides in Fort Hood, Texas, with my own family.

Debbie married five more times after Allae and is now seeking her sixth divorce. She still lives at home in Northwest, Washington, DC Mama died prematurely of heart failure at forty-seven years of age.

Bev married a construction contractor and moved to Kentucky, and Tandy is a single mother of four still living in Washington, DC.

I am no longer in love with Allae. I am in love with Fred. Fred tells me that Allae is still in Japan where he was last stationed with his new family. I hope to someday see him again. Although he will probably never know it, he was the first bandit of my youthful heart, and I will forever cherish those memories.

* * *

Fred entered the room and sat down by the tree with Asa and me. As Asa gave him a big hug and curled up on his lap, he kissed her hair softly and gently touched the small wings of a frosted angel. He then said, "Allae gave you a special gift. Even when the lights flash out, I can still see the angels."

As for Allae and me, many lights had flashed out in our lives, but we never ceased to move forward. In spite of all the setbacks in our lives, we could still see the angels.

A Frosty Summer

"*Yahoooooo*! *Yahoooooo*! School is out, and summer's finally here!" That is all you could hear in the little town of Beam-Ray, just off Co-co-nut Way.

Little Suny looked forward to a long bright summer in the little town of Beam-Ray, just off of Co-co-nut Way.

Suny was visiting Grandma and Grandpa while waiting to go into third grade back in a small neighborhood in Baltimore. Suny was autistic, a condition that caused him to keep his things orderly. He gathered that was probably why he sat cozily in the small closet of his room and rearranging his shoes in an orderly line. Or was it because he was excited about his summer vacation? He felt a little bit confused. Still, he felt happy, and he tended to fumble around when he was happy.

This was his first time staying in Beam-Ray for the whole summer. Summers here were always said to be hotter than anywhere else in the entire world.

Some even believed that the sun came out at night and talked to children. When Suny went to bed, he laughed himself to sleep at such a ridiculous notion. Everyone knew that the sun could not shine at night, or it would never get dark. Everyone in the little town of Beam-Ray, just off Co-co-nut Way, knew that the sun could not talk. Why, that was absurd!

It was 10:00 PM, the creaky old house was settled, and Suny was almost fast asleep except for a few tosses and a few turns. Suddenly, Sunny jumped!

Out of nowhere, there was a soft tap on his bedroom window. Suny was drenched in sweat. It was scorching hot—hotter than it had ever been before.

And it was daytime as well. Yanking back his covers,Suny jumped to his feet, and there it was. Suny peered through his bedroom window and saw a huge yellow ball.

"Who are you?" asked Suny in a frightened voice.

"Who am I? Who am I?" answered the ball. "Why,

Suny, I'm the sun. I am surprised you didn't know that.

We see each other every day. Every day, I look at the children of Beam-Ray, just off Co-co-nut Way. They laugh, play, and enjoy me every day, just like you do."

Suny was puzzled. Why was the sun telling him all of these?

"Why are you telling me all of these, and why did you choose me to visit this morning?" asked Suny.

"I'm telling you because I like you," said the sun.

"I like you because you have almost the same name as me. You can just call me Sunny. And by the way," added Sunny, "it is not morning yet. It is ten o'clock at night."

Confused, Suny peeped and peered through his bedroom window again. "But it is daylight outside," he insisted.

"Well," said Sunny, "that is in my nature, you know.

They don't call me Sunny for nothing. I tend to bring sunshine wherever I go. I also bring heat. Didn't you notice that your pajamas are drenched with sweat?"

Suny looked down at his bedclothes. They were indeed soaked. As Suny looked back up, Sunny continued, "Anyhow, I have come to leave a message with you for the little children of Beam-Ray, just off Co-co-nut Way. Please tell them that I am sorry for the inconvenience, but I have hung around for seventy-four krwikklion years watching them swim, play catch, ride bikes, surf, race, and have picnics on my sunny days."

Sunny looked exhausted.

"Not once," complained Sunny, "not once did anyone ever just look up to the sky, and say to me, 'Thank you, Mr. Sunny, for all of the beautiful sunshine in which you have allowed us to have a good time.'"

Sunny looked very sad as he continued with his message.

"I fear that I have been taken for granted by all of the children of Beam-Ray, just off Co-co-nut Way.

Therefore, I have decided to go on vacation to a make-believe land until you all learn to appreciate me.

Because I am leaving when you need me most, during the summer vacation, you will just have to manage without fun this summer or find a substitute sun.

Let's see how you all like it when my archrival, Old Boy Winter, takes over. He and the moon work together. For years, he and I have competed when it came to providing nice weather for the children of Beam-Ray, just off Co-co-nut Way. As we all know, I have won that competition. No one wants to be cold all of the time, and we all just love sunlight. You and the children of Beam-Ray, just off Co-co-nut Way, cannot do without me. You have been spoiled by my generosity. You will be sorry that you took me for granted for all these years." With that, Sunny fled far, far away. Suny was almost in tears.

"Come back, Sunny," he yelled. "What will we do without you? You are not allowed to go on vacation.

Whoever heard of the sun going on vacation? We need you. What will I tell my dear friends of Beam-Ray, just off Co-co-nut Way?"

But Sunny was nowhere to be found. He must not have heard anything that Suny said. Suny walked sadly back to his bed, rubbing his teary eyes. He removed the pillowcases from his two pillows and put them all in a neat little row. *The sun is gone, and our s*ummer is ruined. Oh, why did we ever take Sunny for *granted?* Suny wondered. After all, the sun has feelings too.

As Sunny soared farther and farther away, it began to get darker and colder. Soon, Suny heard the voices of the children of Beam-Ray, just off Co-co-nut Way as they gathered in the streets in the early morning. In the darkness, Suny felt for his robe and coat, found them, and ran outside yelling, "We all have been taking the sun for granted. He went on vacation!"

"Vacation!" yelled the children. "He cannot do that, we need him."

"Yeah, but where were we when he needed us?" Suny asked.

Everything got quiet. Then Winnie, the wisest girl on the block, replied, "Okay, he's on vacation. Now we must decide how to get him back."

The children of Beam-Ray, just off Co-co-nut Way, sat up under thick quilts on the cold browning grass as they listened to Old Boy Winter laughing and blowing them with all of his might. He was certainly willing to take over for Sunny. The children of Beam-Ray, just off Co-co-nut Way, rocked back and forth as they tried to figure out what to do. Suny thought extra hard. Then it finally came to him.

"I have it!" yelled Suny. "We will all stand outside shouting 'thank you' for a long time and hope that Sunny hears us and decides to come back."

"Why, that is ridiculous," snapped Winnie sharply.

"Why should we stand around yelling out here in this cold weather, making our voices hoarse, and freezing our toes?"

Many of the other children began nodding their heads in agreement with Winnie.

"Suny," said Winnie, pointing at Suny, "you are the one who spoke to the sun, so you need to come up with a better solution. We are all depending on you."

All the children again nodded in agreement. "We are all waiting," said Winnie as they began to walk away to return to their nice, comfortable, warm homes.

"Suny," yelled Winnie over her shoulder, "you better come up with an answer before everyone starts to get up in the morning. After all, we do not want to let everyone know that our sun has gone on vacation.

What will people think of us if they know that we have been taking the sun for granted?"

Winnie turned back and walked away with the other children. Suny looked disillusioned. How in the world could he come up with a solution? He could not make the sun come back if the sun did not care to return. He knew he couldn't rise up in the sky to search for the sun. There were just no answers, yet all of the children of Beam-Ray, just off Co-co-nut Way, were counting on him for help. Suny went quietly back to his bedroom to think about what they could do.

He quietly lay down on his small comfortable bed made of fresh pine cones and gray goose feathers. It was cold, so he pulled a fuzzy quilt over his little body and began to think. Before he knew it, he was startled awake by a rough tap on his bedroom window. He was so very happy! "Sunny's back! Sunny's back," little Suny yelled as he ran for his bedroom window.

As he ran, Suny noticed that somehow the window tap did not seem as soft and pleasant as Sunny's first tap before he went on vacation. Suny stooped down and peeped curiously over the windowsill to see Sunny.

Where was all of the sunlight and heat that Sunny produced? he wondered. Suny suddenly felt a sharp, bone-stinging wind as his room was highlighted with a dull bluish glow. At the same moment, Suny saw a big pushed-in face peer into his window.

"Who are you?" asked Suny, a little frightened.

"Who am I? Who am I?" repeated the face on the window. "Why, Suny, I'm the moon. I am surprised that you did not know that. Just call me Moony."

Moony looked quite pleased as he said, "I have watched the children of Beam-Ray, just off Co-co-nut Way, play and have fun in the sun for seventy-four krwikklion years now. Oh, how they love the summer, especially when school is out, but I'm afraid that Old Boy Winter is suffering. Everyone ignores him."

Suny was puzzled. How could one ignore the winter?

"How can anyone ignore the winter?" asked Suny, speaking his thoughts out loud. "Everyone knows that you have fun in the summertime, but stay inside during the winter, drinking hot chocolate and watching television."

Moony looked upset with Suny. "Oh, how wrong you are, Suny," said Moony. "Come with me." At that moment, Moony extended a long moonbeam, which lifted Suny's window and picked him up. Moony took Suny for a soaring, exciting ride across the skies on the moonbeam. It was heavenly, and Suny loved it. It was his first tour of the sky. He absolutely could not wait to see what Moony had to show him. They soared over oceans, night clouds, and cosmic junk.

They passed the Big Dipper, the Little Dipper, the North Star, and the planet Neptune. They rode over the Earth until they reached a huge grayish-blue ball of what appeared to Suny to be old swiss cheese and candy wax. Moony shifted his moondust beams and suddenly dumped Suny into the cheese-wax alongside himself. Inside, it was cold and dim, but pleasant.

Suny could see Winnie, himself, and the rest of their friends playing outside through the ball. It was wintertime. They were skiing on snow-covered hills, building snowmen, and throwing snowballs. Suny watched as they camped out under the moon, snuggling into thick warm quilts by dancing campfires while toasting marshmallows under the pretty blue moonlight. Suny and his friends were singing Christmas carols, ice-skating, and building igloos.

Suny threw his head back in laughter. He had never had so much fun, not even in a happy town like Baltimore. Suny had never realized how much fun the winter could be until Sunny had gone on vacation. It was fantastic.

At that point, Moony shone a beautiful moon glow into Suny's eyes.

"You see now, Suny?" Moony said. "It does not have to be summer for children to have fun. Old Boy Winter can really show you all a good time if you just let him.

"I'll tell you what," continued Moony, "I will shine for the sun until he returns. As we speak, I have arranged for your friends from Beam-Ray, just off Co-co-nut Way, to watch us on video television, so they know what is going on. Later on, we may just have to give the town some type of catchy winter name. From now on, the little town of Beam-Ray, just off Co-co-nut Way, will always enjoy the winter, and should Sunny come back, I ask that you all remember the winter and use it for fun just as you do the summer."

"Thanks," said Suny, shaking an outstretched moonbeam. "We will."

Suny had a great adventure, but now was quite tired. He sincerely hoped that his friends in Beam-Ray, just off Co-co-nut Way, had enjoyed the winter scene just as much as he had. He would go home full of great winter ideas. Who needed Sunny?

Their winter vacation could be just as much fun. Suny closed his eyes, yawned, stretched, and began to speak. "Moony," he said, "I am tired now, could you please take me back to . . ."

Suny opened his eyes. Somehow, he was back in his own bedroom. He heard a small tap at his bedroom window. Suny was drenched with sweat.

He saw it was glowing like diamonds outside his bedroom window. Suny smiled as he went to the window and looked out.

"Hello, Sunny."

"How'd ya know it was me?" said Sunny with a yellowish smile.

"Why, Sunny," said Suny, "I'm surprised that you didn't know that you tend to bring sunshine wherever you go. Anyhow, for eight years now, the children of Beam-Ray, just off Co-co-nut Way, have watched you sit back and enjoy the free shows, time, and attention that they have allowed you. Not once, not once, did they ever get a thank you. If you ever go on vacation again, we will enjoy winter and only winter for as long as we please."

Suny looked out and saw all the children of Beam-

Ray, just off Co-co-nut Way, standing around his bedroom window smiling and nodding in agreement.

He felt really confident.

"You saw the video, just like the rest of us, didn't you, Sunny?" asked Winnie.

"Yes," said Sunny sadly, "and I promise to never go on vacation again."

"And do you give your word that you will not try to interfere when winter comes, and we enjoy it just as we do the summer sun?"

"Yes, I will share you with winter," said Sunny sorrowfully to the children of Beam-Ray, just off Co-co—nut Way.

All the children laughed and apologized for taking Sunny for granted. Sunny smiled also and apologized for taking them for granted as well. Still, he had found a new friend in Moony.

Suny was happy too. From then on, every time he visited his grandparents during the summer, he saw Sunny and Moony passing by each other at dusk and dawn, laughing and shaking hands in the sky. They had finally learned to share the children of the little town of Beam-Ray, just off Co-co-nut Way.

My Last Party

I can still remember crunching through the snow in my new rubber boots as Mama and I walked up the steps to our large Washington DC home. Like in so many other homes, the loud rock-and-roll music boomed through every crack. The downtown city bus that we had just exited, cooing about the movies, had hardly turned the corner before Mama informed me that I was to go straight to bed as soon as we entered the house. She had loaned the living room to my cousin,Margaret, to throw some type of crazy holiday party.

Margaret had already informed me, "You have to be sixteen to be invited." I was only twelve years old, too young. But that wasn't going to keep me from sneaking to my first party, and that's what I did as soon as Mama fell asleep.

When the long skinny hand had slowly gone around the entire clock once, I hopped out of bed, tiptoed downstairs, sneaked into the living room, and crouched down between two small pulled-together love seats. Through the narrow crack, I could hazily see the entire living room.

Through dimmed lights, I saw that the room was full of many, many teenagers. A black leather couch faced me and matched my hiding place. Beside the couch was a wooden walnut-colored stereo box with black fishnet speakers on each side of it.

Sitting in a squatting position, I pressed my back hard against the pink carnation wallpaper and peered out. I was just thinking about how great it was to finally be at a party when I spotted it—a huge dome-shaped, transparent object with a lot of different colored little balls inside. There were green, yellow, pink, blue, orange, red, purple, brown, and white ones. What was this strange object that rested on a stack of small records on top of the stereo?

I could also see what seemed to be hundreds of pairs of blurred, swaying feet moving fast, in time with the music. Everywhere, there were bongos, oxfords, and blue-tipped sneakers. There were rolled white bobby socks and black-and-brown loafers with bright shinny pennies in them. People were hopping and leaping on and off of the floor. Why was all of this jumping and leaping going on? Was the floor on fire or something? I reached down and began to check the floor for heat. I ran my fingertips across the rough sweaty-cool wooden surface. Its dark mahogany surface had been badly marked from corner to corner with huge maplike black stains. A pair of thick, dark pink potato-sack curtains hung limply and loose on top of the dingy white windowsill behind the sofa.

A half bottle of Lotta Cola and a small white poster that said "We come 61" were halfway hidden the windowsill behind the curtains.

I was sitting very still in my hiding place and just enjoying the music, the cha-cha, and the limbo-rock when I suddenly noticed a huge bunch of different colored balls with long white tails dangling from them, flying then popping in midair. After the pop, shriveled-up piles of lazy rubber, with the same type of tail as the balls, would plop lifelessly to the floor. Someone yelled "Hello 61" and began to sing something about old lake zine. Then there was a loud echoed fizz and a small bit of some strange liquid splashed into my open mouth. It felt like heavy salt, pepper, and spices on my thirsty tongue. All at once, a loud siren went off, and the room went pitch-black, then red, then black, then blue, then black, then purple, then black, then green.

All the leapers turned into mechanical-moving robots, some real, and some as black pictures on the wall.

Some were massive creatures. Others were small ones. I was sure they were out to get me. Fleeing from hiding place between the love seats, I ran smack into the security of Mama's warm arms. She had come looking for me. As I slept in Mama's arms that night, I could not help but dream about my last party!

To Subtract a Gwzzkk?

(A story of subtraction)

He is huge, about eight feet tall! He is dark, fat, and hairy with long, green, pointed teeth that drip with brown goo. His long black claws are pencil sharp, and he has gigantic bloodred eyes that flash and flicker like fire when he gets upset. He is so mean that he can freeze entire oceans with one breath. His name is Mr. Gwzzkk.

Little Six leaped up from his small elegant bed. He stared wide-eyed at his white satin covers and beautiful bed made of fresh honeycombs held together by sweet Spanish molasses. Sweat poured from him as he remembered his nightmare. Yes, indeed, he had been dreaming about the Gwzzkk. The Gwzzkk had to be passed to get from Little Six's apartment to his good friend Little Nine's. Little Six had never actually met the Gwzzkk. No one had. All he knew about the Gwzzkk was that he was a gross scary creature that lived on the way to Little Nine's. For this reason, Little Six could not visit Little Nine.

Little Six looked out of his bedroom window. The sun had finally managed to sneak past the dawn, and lo and behold, it was a brand new day. And what a beautiful day it was too! Little Six lived with his mom and dad on the bottom floor in the back of the Subtraction Apartment building. Next door to Little Six lived Little One. Directly above Little Six lived Little Four. Next door to Little Four lived Little Nine. Directly below Little Nine lived Little One. Their apartment building looked like this:

9	4
1	6
Front	Back

Last season, Little Six had been upset because he had run out of eggs, which he needed to grow his eggplant. He needed to borrow six eggs in order to grow his eggplant, but he knew the house rules. There could be no borrowing until the borrowing season came around. This was the first day of the borrowing season.

"Bottom back, bottom back," Little Six kept repeating as he put on fresh clothes. He knew the rule. The bottom back number was always to be the first in the building to borrow. The bottom front number came next. The upstairs numbers were not allowed to borrow at all.

They were the ones that the bottom numbers had to borrow from. Little Six knew the rules. He was only supposed to borrow from the number living directly over him.

After getting dressed and preparing his little borrowing basket lined with a large folded bear-fur cloth, Little Six was so happy that he began to hum as he started upstairs to Little Four's house to borrow six eggs. Now what could possibly go wrong on a beautiful day like this? he thought. He soon found out.

Little Six went upstairs and knocked on Little Four's door. Little Four eased her door open and poked her tiny little head out. When she saw Little Six's borrowing basket, she replied, "Why, Little Six, I'm surprised at you. You know the rules. And because your name is Six, you are only allowed to borrow six items. And because my name is Four, I am only allowed to lend out four items. If you can make me a bigger number, I can help you."

Little Six sighed. He had totally forgotten that Little Four was smaller. He could not borrow from a number smaller than himself. Still, he knew the rule. He had to be the first to borrow since he was the bottom back number. If he waited, he would hold up the bottom front number, his friend Little One. Little One had to go upstairs to borrow in two days. Little Six was flushed and upset. There was only one thing left to do. He had to go next door to Little Nine's apartment and borrow six eggs. But how in the world could he get past that Gwzzkk he had heard so much about?

Yelling good luck to Little Six, Little Four eased her door shut. Little Six trembled, took a deep breath, and started next door to Little Nine's apartment. Maybe he could be extra quiet and sneak past the Gwzzkk without being seen. At first, it seemed to be working, but just as soon as Little Six stepped over the red borrowing line in order to get to Little Nine's door, it happened. There were two loud sizzles! Little Six leaped back, only to land on a huge black furry creature. He felt a large creepy body pin him down to the dusty floor so tightly that he could not breathe.

Beads of perspiration flew everywhere as Little Six gasped for breath, desperately fighting to free himself from whatever had him pinned down.

"Mr. Gwzzkk," he yelled, "please let me go!" There was no answer. "What are you?" shouted Little Six, struggling to get free.

"I am whatever you choose me to be," answered a hoarse, husky voice seemingly out of nowhere.

""Well, what I choose you to be is gone," yelled Little Six.

"As you wish," said the voice and then faded away into silence.

Little Six looked up. The furry bear cloth with which he had lined his basket was sticking to his nose.

Little Nine leaped up from off Little Six.

"Sorry that I fell on you Little Six," apologized Little Nine. "I know that I am quite heavy. I weigh nine pounds. I could see that it was hard for you to breathe.

You frightened me though. I did not expect you to come to me to borrow. Didn't you hear me making the sizzling sounds? I kept going PSSSST, PSSSST. I was just so happy to see you. You know that you never visit me. I'm really sorry that I fell on top of you when you fell down."

Little Six laughed. "*Gh*, that is all right. I came to borrow six eggs from you and had to get past the Gwzzkk."

"The Gw who?" asked Little Nine.

"Gh, nothing," said Little Six, wondering if the Gwzzkk was really only in his mind.

"Anyway," said Little Nine, "you know the rules, when you borrow from next door to your upstairs neighbor, you are only allowed to borrow one."

"Thanks," said Little Six, taking that one. "I will try to visit you more often." They waved good-bye as Little Six walked across the hall to Little Four's door. Little Nine was not so heavy anymore. She had given away one, so she was now Little Eight.

Because he knew the rule, he knocked on Little Four's door, put the one in front of her, and watched her become Little Fourteen. He had made her larger.

Little Six then borrowed the six eggs from Little Fourteen. Because the new Little Fourteen had just given away six eggs, she was no longer Little Fourteen, but another Little Eight, just like her next door neighbor.

Little Six took the six eggs back downstairs to his apartment and grew a very tasty eggplant. Two days later, he watched Little One go upstairs to borrow a peanut butter sandwich from the newly made LittleEight just above her in order to start a peanut butter factory. Mr. Gwzzkk never came back. Little Six would not let him.

CPSIA information can be obtained at www.ICGtesting.com
Printed in the USA
LVOW11*2325161113

361612LV00002B/104/P